"Hello there…"

His heart bounced.

"Oh! You've put my bags in already. Thanks so much. Sorry I wasn't here. I had to go and splash my face. It was so warm in the plane…"

He stared down at his hands, heart clanging. The voice was familiar. Achingly familiar. But it couldn't be. No. It was surely just the acoustics under the canopy, or his mind playing tricks because he was hot and bothered and overwrought. *Get a grip*. He drew in a breath and turned around.

See! Blond hair. Short. Not dark red and endless like… And mirror shades weren't Maddie's style… His mouth dried. But that nose… His heart bucked. And those lips… His lungs were emptying out, collapsing. He reached for the canopy frame, gripping it hard, trying to make the face he was looking at not fit the memory, but her hand was going to her sunglasses, slowly drawing them down, and his pulse was hammering in his ears, seismic waves rising and falling beneath his feet. It was absolutely, unequivocally, 100 percent her.

"Oh my God…" Her eyes were filling. "Kaden…?"

Dear Reader,

Welcome to my sixth book for Harlequin Romance!

A couple of years ago, I was lucky enough to spend a short time at a gorgeous private game reserve close to the South African/Botswanan border. As soon as I stepped into my tented lodge, with its vast canopied bed and wraparound veranda, I knew that I'd found the perfect setting for another romance. Many of the things I saw and experienced for myself have made it into this story—for example, Madeleine's first encounter with the elephants, including the posturing bull, and the general views, sights and sounds of the bushveld. Other story elements are pure fiction. A certain scene on the front seat of the safari vehicle comes to mind.

The inspiration has somewhat tawdry roots, insofar as Madeleine's father is a sleazy politician, but what I really wanted to explore was the impact of her father's scandalous crimes not only on Madeleine but on Kaden and their wider families too, heightened suitably for dramatic effect.

I hope that you love reading Madeleine and Kaden's emotional reunion story and that you enjoy your stay at Masoka as much as I enjoyed my own game reserve experience at Madikwe.

Ella x

Recycling programs
for this product may
not exist in your area.

ISBN-13: 978-1-335-73679-6

Their Surprise Safari Reunion

Copyright © 2022 by Ella Hayes

For questions and comments about the quality of this book, please contact us at CustomerService@Harlequin.com.

Harlequin Enterprises ULC
22 Adelaide St. West, 41st Floor
Toronto, Ontario M5H 4E3, Canada
www.Harlequin.com

Printed in U.S.A.

Their Surprise Safari Reunion

Ella Hayes

After ten years as a television camerawoman, **Ella Hayes** started her own photography business so that she could work around the demands of her young family. As an award-winning wedding photographer, she's documented hundreds of love stories in beautiful locations, both at home and abroad. She lives in central Scotland with her husband and two grown-up sons. She loves reading, traveling with her camera, running and great coffee.

Books by Ella Hayes

Her Brooding Scottish Heir
Italian Summer with the Single Dad
Unlocking the Tycoon's Heart
Tycoon's Unexpected Caribbean Fling
The Single Dad's Christmas Proposal

Visit the Author Profile page at Harlequin.com.

For Steven and Adeline. Thank you for Madikwe.

Praise for
Ella Hayes

CHAPTER ONE

'LINA…? HEY! MS JAMES!'

She jerked awake, heart thumping, trying to locate the strange voice in her head, and then a cream cabin came into focus followed by windows full of blue sky and wispy streaks of cloud. *Of course!* She was airborne, strapped into the tiny, noisy plane that was taking her to Masoka, and the voice in her head wasn't in her head at all, but was coming through the headset she was wearing, or rather, half wearing. Must have slipped while she was sleeping. She straightened it and looked up.

Steve, the pilot, was eyeing her over his shoulder, his aviators glinting. 'Sorry to wake you but we're starting our descent shortly and it could be bumpy. There's a ridge up ahead. The air currents on the other side can be lively.'

'You mean hairy!'

He grinned. 'I prefer lively.'

'Whatever.' She held in a smile. 'Thanks for the heads-up!'

'Anytime!' He turned forwards, flicking a switch on the panel. 'Just don't drop off again, okay? You need to be awake for landing...'

In case of emergencies was what he wasn't saying, but she knew the script. She was a seasoned traveller after all, a seasoned sleeper on planes, and trains, and buses. Sleeping at night, in an actual bed, was the thing she couldn't do. She touched the mic. 'Roger that!'

A chuckle filled her ears followed by an empty hiss. He was speaking to someone else now, probably checking in with the airstrip.

She pulled the cans off and stretched, swallowing a yawn, then looked down at the *bushveld*. Vast. Green. Empty. She felt her heart expanding. It was perfect! Perfect place, perfect time! She wasn't a lucky person—far from it—but she'd felt lucky that morning four months ago when Fran Palmer's email had landed in her in-box...

Lina, I know you're in demand and probably already booked, but we're opening Masoka Safari Lodge at the beginning of February and a write-up on your fantastic blog would really help to put us on the map. If you could fit us in for a week early in the month, we promise to give

you plenty to write about: game drives, hot-air ballooning, a night under canvas at our luxury bush camp followed by a river cruise at dawn. But it's not only a ringside seat to the Big Five we're offering! At Masoka you can expect the finest cuisine, the finest rooms and the finest facilities—including our relaxing spa and infinity pool. In short, we are offering the ultimate luxury safari experience. We would love the opportunity to welcome you to our world...

She *had* been booked but reshuffling her plans for Fran Palmer had been a no-brainer, not because she was desperate to see the Big Five, or to cruise along an African river at dawn, but because Masoka Safari Lodge was six thousand miles away from London and being six thousand miles away from London in the week that her scumbag father was being released from jail had suddenly felt like the best idea she'd never had.

And now she was here, flying deeper and deeper into the back of beyond, feeling freer and lighter with every mile. She drew in a slow breath, watching the plane's shadow rippling over the grass, shimmering across a stretch of silver water. Here were hills starting, golden slopes strewn with giant boulders and, winding through them, narrow paths. *Animal tracks?*

She chewed the edge of her lip. Kaden would have known. He'd been mad about animals, and wildlife and—

Don't!

But it was too late. He was already shimmering into view, tanned and wet by the lake, his lips twitching with mischief. *'Look, Maddie!'* And then he'd been opening his hands... Only a tadpole, but it had wriggled suddenly, and she'd stumbled backwards, and he'd creased up with laughter, eyes shining into hers like molten copper...

Kaden...

Why couldn't she let the memories go, memories that always sprouted questions. Was he happy? Married? She touched her travel belt, feeling the tug of the phone inside it. Tracking him down on social media would be easy; after all, he was heir to the Barr retail empire! Maybe he was CEO now, although, *no*, he hadn't wanted that, not at seventeen anyway. Back then, he'd had his heart set on becoming a vet. He'd been busy applying to universities when— *Stop!*

Vet... CEO... Starship trooper! It was academic. She couldn't look. She'd promised herself years ago not to. It would only have been a torment. Besides, looking couldn't turn the clock back. She and Kaden were history, had

been from the moment her mother had bundled her onto the Eurostar all those years ago. No goodbyes. No contact allowed. *God!* How he must have hated her for leaving like that, for not sending word... She felt her heart twisting. But she'd had to do it...for Mum...because everything had been falling apart, and Mum had been worried about the press and phone hacking. Mum had only been trying to protect her, but knowing it hadn't made it any easier to bear, hadn't stopped her crying her heart out for Kaden every day for months and months...

And then after her father was jailed, it had come to her that she couldn't contact him. Hearing him say that he couldn't be associated with her any more would have crushed her all over again because that's what he would have said. How could he have said anything else? The Barrs were good people with an impeccable business reputation whereas her father, Peter Saint James—treasury minister and so-called pillar of society—had been sent down for corruption and conspiracy to perjure.

She felt her stomach shrivelling. Because of *him* she was tainted. Because of *him* she'd had to disappear, had had to change her name and her appearance so she wouldn't be hounded. She'd had to start a whole new life, and she'd done it, hadn't she, made a life for herself that was hers to control, except... She felt tears prickling, burning behind her lids. She wasn't in control. She was running away again because of *him*, this time because of his bloody book, the memoir he'd written in jail that was somehow already a *Sunday Times* bestseller before either he or it had been released! What was he doing it for: money, notoriety? Didn't he have enough of both already? Didn't he ever stop to think about the effect on her and on Mum, or didn't he care? *God!* If only *she* could make herself not care, could make herself not feel ashamed every waking second of her life!

She leaned her forehead against the window. *Enough!* Self-pity never helped. She needed to focus on the positive. Yes, her father was a sleazebag, but Mum was a rock. And *Destination Heaven* was a success, the number-one luxury travel blog on the circuit, and the blogging life was far more interesting and sustainable than the modelling career she'd had to abandon. Even better, it kept her moving. *Safe...*

As for Kaden... Muss-haired and laughing by the lake, pulling her up again, his eyes all aglow... She blinked the image away. Of course he was in her head, and *yes*, in her heart too, still, but it was probably like that for everyone with their first love. *First lover!* The feeling never left. That feeling of not being able to breathe, of not wanting to be even an inch away... It had felt like that with him. It had felt like for ever. She swallowed hard. But they'd been kids. What had they known about anything? Just because it had felt real didn't mean they'd have necessarily stayed tog—

The plane pitched suddenly, throwing her sideways, then it waltzed, creaking and straining. She pressed herself into her seat, bracing for the next judder. She wasn't scared. If anything, she was glad. The plane had jolted her back to the present, the all-important now. She turned to watch the ground see-sawing closer, the bright green bushes and the red brown earth. The past was dust. Kaden and Maddie were long gone. In the all-important now she was Lina James, award-winning travel writer, and yes, admittedly she was ever so slightly on the run, but she was also about to throw herself headlong into her first ever ultimate luxury safari experience. On balance, maybe it wasn't all bad.

Kaden felt the Jeep slide as he took the bend. *Too fast!* What had his grandmother used to say? *Better to be five minutes late in this world than five minutes too early in the next...* He spun the wheel, straightening, then accelerated hard, squinting through the tangle of grass and bushes, trying to see the airstrip. Grandmother

Barr's wisdom was all very well, but it didn't mean that being late was okay, especially when the person you were late for was, according to Fran, the queen of the elite travel scene. *Fran!* His chest went tight. *She* wouldn't have been late. She'd have had it all under control, but he absolutely couldn't think about Fran right now. She was gone, and he was… *Oh, God!* He was in trouble! The Piper was already parked, its doors open. He eased his foot off the accelerator, scouring the tarmac, heart thumping. There was Steve, helping someone out of the plane. Lina James! And she was probably already marking Masoka down for the lack of a welcome party!

Damn!

He refocused on the road and pressed on, feeling a dead weight sinking. If he'd sent Jerry to check on the wild dog pups that morning, instead of going himself, he'd have been here on time. The problem was, when it came to animals, he was useless at delegating. It wasn't sentimentality. Vets couldn't afford to be sentimental! The ten pups wouldn't all survive, he knew that, but knowing it didn't make them any less compelling, and it was compulsion that drove him, a sense of mission. Without that passion, without that compulsion to watch, and monitor, and protect animals, particularly the endangered species like the wild dogs, then he'd have had no business buying Masoka Game Reserve in the first place! No, he wasn't going to beat himself up for putting the animals first. Bottom line, the frilly, romantic, safari side of the business only interested him in so far as it was going to fund his conservation operations and his second-phase plans. But it wasn't going to fund anything without wealthy punters, and here he was, arriving late to pick up the very person who could deliver them!

He barrelled through the entrance, rattling over the cattle grid, then touched the brake. Screeching up in a spray of grit wouldn't do. It would make him seem chaotic, and chaos was not what he was selling at Masoka. He drew in a steadying breath and coasted sedately over to the plane. Two fat leather holdalls squatted under the shade of the wing; Lina's, presumably, but where was she? And where was Steve? He killed the engine and twisted to look back at the small, thatched building that the pilots jokingly called 'the terminal.' Maybe Steve was showing Ms James the facilities!

He parked his shades on the dash and jumped down. Maybe it was better this way, being alone for a few moments. It meant he could catch his breath—*calm the hell down*—and get her bags loaded.

He swung them into the back, leaning in to wedge them so they wouldn't roll. Not that he any intention of driving back like a lunatic! *No!* He was going to take it easy, spin it out, take the opportunity to schmooze—

'Hello there...'

His heart bounced.

'Oh! You've put my bags in already. Thanks so much. Sorry I wasn't here. I had to go and splash my face. It was so warm in the plane...'

He stared down at his hands, heart clanging. The voice was familiar. Achingly familiar. But it couldn't be. *No.* It was surely just the acoustics under the canopy, or his mind playing tricks because he was hot and bothered and overwrought. *Get a grip.* He drew in a breath and turned round.

See! Blond hair. Short. Not dark red and endless like... And mirror shades weren't Maddie's style... His mouth dried. But that nose... His heart bucked. And those lips... His lungs were emptying out, collapsing. He reached for the canopy frame, gripping it hard, trying to make the face he was looking at not fit the memory, but her hand was going to her sunglasses, slowly drawing them down, and his pulse was hammering in his ears, seismic waves rising and falling beneath his feet, and he couldn't skew the pieces out of sync no matter how hard he tried because it was *her* blue eyes fastening on his, *her* luscious mouth falling open. It was absolutely, unequivocally, one hundred percent *her*.

'Oh, my God...' Her eyes were filling. 'Kaden...?'

'Madeleine!' It came out as a mangled whisper, but he couldn't help that. His throat was a desert. Was she really here, the girl he'd once loved more than life itself? He gulped a breath. What to say, how to feel? So much history, so many exploding emotions. There wasn't enough space for it, no way of gathering it together into any kind of order, especially when there was this wave of pure joy rising, engulfing the rest, propelling his legs forwards and then somehow—*how?*—his arms were going around her and she was melting in like she'd used to do a lifetime ago, and for a piece of a second nothing was broken, nothing else mattered, but then her body stiffened and she was pulling away, and just like that the wave collapsed.

'I'm sorry... I'm...' She was breathing in bursts, twisting her fingers into the legs of her sunglasses. 'I wasn't expecting this...' Her eyes came to his. 'I mean, *you*...'

His heart crashed. Of course she hadn't been expecting him. If she'd known he was here she wouldn't have come, would she, not if the past

twelve years were anything to go by. And yet…
she'd folded into his arms so easily and the
warmth he'd felt flowing from her had felt real
and deep and familiar. Way to confuse himself,
hugging her like that, opening himself up to
whatever. He should have resisted the impulse,
fought a bit harder instead of caving in a heartbeat. Seemed that old habits did die hard. He'd
need to watch himself.

He pushed a hand through his hair, collect-
ing himself. 'I wasn't expecting you either. I
was expecting—'

'Lina James.' She seemed to shrink into herself. 'I changed my name a long time ago. Had
to, after everything…'

Of course she'd have done that. *Of course!*
That was why he'd never managed to find her
on social media. All that searching. Friends,
friends of friends, every oblique connection.
Meanwhile the name she'd devised was a simple
distillation: Lina James from Madeleine Saint
James. At twenty he might have picked up on it
but when Fran had started talking about email-
ing Lina James regarding a feature on *Destination Heaven*, he hadn't thought a thing about it
except that if she could pull it off, then it would
extend their reach far beyond the press coverage
she'd already lined up. And she *had* pulled it off.

He swallowed hard. But now Fran was gone,

and Lina James was standing in front of him, except that she was really Madeleine—*Mad-die*—taking him apart with her eyes, making him feel...what? *Oh, God!* Why couldn't he pin a single feeling down? All he could do was look at her.

There were hollows under her cheekbones now, tiny lines at the corners of her eyes, but the freckles over her nose were the same. They matched her hair, not this hair but the dark red hair he'd loved to fold into his hands and let slip through his fingers, the hair that had bounced and tumbled its way across billboards and television screens for Tresses Organix.

He pressed a finger along his eyebrow chasing an ache. 'You changed your hair too...'

'Yes.' A wan smile ghosted across her lips. 'It was kind of recognisable...'

Famous hair. *Of course!* And then before he could stop them familiar words were lining up on his tongue, flying free on the wings of his famously terrible mid-Atlantic accent. 'Turn their heads with Tresses Organix!'

A smile broke her face apart, switching the light back on and all the lovely radiance he remembered. And then she was giggling, dropping her shoulder, doing the advert. 'Go on...' One flirty eyebrow went up. 'You know you want to!'

He felt laughter vibrating, warmth rushing in. *Maddie. Mads.* Beneath the peroxide she was still there, the same. *Still beautiful.* He smiled. 'You've still got it, you know!'

'Thank you.' Her eyes held him for a moment and then her lips quirked. 'Sadly your voice-over still sucks...'

He felt a pang, a sudden unbearable itch in his fingers, because in the before this would have been his cue. She'd have been giggling, teasing him with her eyes, and he'd have dived for her, making her squeal, catching her wrists, pinning her body with his, and then there'd have been that sublime moment when the tempo changed, that moment when everything softened, and her hands would have wound into his hair, and her lips would have come to his and—

Don't!

He drove his hands into his pockets hard. Sliding backwards was a seriously bad idea. He couldn't go there, couldn't waken all the slumbering details. It was the now that mattered, how to deal with—

'Kaden...?' He blinked her back into focus, felt his heart skip the way it had never skipped for Fran. 'What do we do now?' A shadow lengthened behind her gaze. 'What I mean is, do you want me to stay?'

His chest went tight. Did he? Gut reaction: he

didn't want her to go, but could he handle her staying? Could his heart handle it? *Oh, God!* He needed to find his voice before the space between them filled up with hesitation, but the only thing surfacing was a question of his own, somewhat disingenuous, but then hadn't he earned the right to be that at least? He swallowed hard. 'Why wouldn't I want you to stay?'

For a moment her expression was incredulous, and then her lips pressed together, tears mounting from the lower lids of her eyes. 'Because...'

He felt his heart contracting, an unwelcome drop of bitterness expanding. *Because* after the Peter Saint James scandal broke, she'd vanished without a word, even though she was supposed to have loved him. *Because* in twelve whole years she'd never messaged, emailed or sent him so much as a sodding postcard! Because now— *now*—she was having an attack of the guilts!

Stop!

Hadn't he just resolved not to slide backwards, and especially, he couldn't let himself slide into bitter waters, not while the fact of her was still sinking in, while the shock of her was still thrumming through his veins. This wasn't the moment to be sifting through old hurts, letting them twist him even more out of shape than he already was. This was a moment for objectivity. Focus. Purpose. He needed her to write that blog post. Yes, courtesy of Fran's brilliant organisational skills, he had a posse of travel journalists on the case, but the reach of *Destination Heaven* was far greater. A glowing endorsement there was going to put him on track to achieve all the things he wanted to achieve at Masoka.

And Masoka was his life, *ergo* Masoka trumped everything, *ergo* she had to stay.

He took a breath and freed his hands from his pockets. 'Maddie, whatever you're thinking, you need to let it go.'

Wetness flooded her gaze. 'But I just—'

'Please. Don't—' His throat closed. Maybe it was selfish cutting her off, but he couldn't let her unravel. If she did, then he'd start unravelling too and what would be the point of that, of pulling all the pain into the foreground for the sake of, what…an apology? *No.* Staying laser focused on the business was the only way he was going to get through the week, so she needed to know that he wasn't looking for explanations or for anything from her except the thing she'd come to do.

He held up his palms. 'Look, just to be clear, I do want you stay, all right, but what I don't want is to…' The words dried on his tongue. 'What I can't do is…' Why couldn't he say it?

Was it because her eyes were gleaming, full of history, tugging his heart out, or was it because what he was trying to say—that he didn't want to get into the past—was only half true after all? *Oh, God!* That was it. He was struggling to get the words out because the words were lies and lying had never been part of their landscape. But how could he possibly open up and tell her that the part of him that wasn't terrified of hearing what she might say was desperate for an explanation, hungry for the closure he'd been denied? Fact was, he couldn't, at least not now. He wasn't nearly strong enough, or level enough. God, right now he could feel the angry ghost of his seventeen-year-old self, rampaging, kicking down the walls in some alternative universe, but in this one, in *this* moment, he needed to find an adult perspective, because whatever he thought he knew, there was so much more that he didn't. He drew her back into focus. It was all there behind her gaze.

And then her gaze was narrowing into his, and her lips were parting. 'You don't want to get into the before, do you? You don't want to go back…' She swallowed. 'Am I getting warm?'

Half warm, half true, but it was a push in the right direction, a way out of the hole he was in.

'Yes, that's exactly what I was failing miserably to say.' He managed a smile and caught an answering warmth in her eyes that bolstered his spirits. 'Look, I'm not trying to be a jerk about it, Mads, but frankly I'm in a state of shock. And so are you, right?' She nodded almost imperceptibly. 'Truth is, I can barely think straight right now so maybe I *am* being a colossal jerk and if that's the case, then I'm sorry.'

'You're not being a jerk. I'm not thinking that at all.' Her hand closed over his forearm for a warm, brief second, and then a light came into her eyes that looked a lot like relief. 'And you're right about the shock.' A corner of her mouth twitched up. 'It's certainly not your average day, is it?'

He felt a smile coming. 'You can say that again.' *One last push.* He ploughed his hands through his hair. 'So, what do you say to us just focusing on the present?'

Her eyebrows flashed. 'Sounds like a plan to me.'

Relief loosened his limbs. It was going to work out. Squaring things away, cleaning off the slate, had been the right move. Now they were on the same page. Now there was a nice safe space for them to move around in.

He slid his hand along the canopy rail. 'Speaking of plans, I hope you're ready to throw yourself into the luxury safari experience.'

'Hmm…' She pressed a finger to her cheek,

waggling her eyebrows. 'Sounds tough but, you know, I'll give it my best shot.'

Maddie! Irresistible when she was playing the clown, irresistible full stop, but he was going to have to resist her, not let all his freshly drawn lines blur.

'Seriously though, I do need you to write a cracking piece about us.' And then suddenly he could feel his own inner clown stirring, a familiar mischievous spark igniting, an urge too compelling to resist. He held in a smile. 'That's assuming you can write as well as that Lina James girl...'

Her face stiffened for a beat, and then she was laughing her rich fruity laugh, her eyes shining. 'Oh, I'm *way* better than her.' She parked her sunglasses on her head, and then her eyebrow slid up in that cute way he remembered. 'Actually, between you and me, she's a bit of a fake!'

CHAPTER TWO

SHE WATCHED HIM walking round and getting in. Same easy gait, same tilt of the head. A tingle shimmered through. Was this really happening? Just twenty minutes ago she'd been stepping on to the tarmac wondering why Fran Palmer wasn't there to meet her, and now she was about to take off into the *veld* with the only boy she'd ever loved, except…he wasn't a boy any more. The broad shoulders he'd had at seventeen were fuller now, their muscular curves all too obvious beneath his shirt. His hair was still thick, still deliciously unkempt, but the smattering of stubble around his jaw was new. Its soft rub had grazed her temple when he'd pulled her into his arms, and she'd wanted to slide her hands upwards and touch it, but then she'd remembered that he wasn't hers to touch, and she'd had to pull away quickly before it got too confusing. Not that it seemed to have helped any. She was still fifty shades of confused, everything reeling and thrumming and skittering, and having him sitting barely two feet away wasn't helping one little bit.

His eyes pinned her suddenly. 'You, okay?'

She felt her heart flip and tumble, a sudden ridiculous urge to laugh. She was many things but *okay* definitely wasn't one of them. She moistened her lips. 'Yes. I was just—' Her mind went blank.

His eyebrows drew in. 'Me too.'

'Me too, what...?'

He shrugged, then lifted a pair of Ray-Bans off the dash. 'I don't know, but isn't that the point?' His lips twitched upwards. 'We're basically not fit for purpose right now.'

She felt a smile filling her cheeks. *Kaden!* No one had ever been able to make her smile the way he could, even now when she was in total disarray...

Whatever you're thinking, you need to let it go...

He'd given her a free pass. *Thank God!* Because just before he'd said it, there'd been something in his eyes that had made her think that in spite of the hug, and in spite of laughing over the Tresses advert, he was going to tell her that she couldn't stay, that he couldn't have anything to do with her. She'd felt her father's shame pulsing through, wanting to spill out in tears, apologies, explanations, anything that would fill in the years and make things right. But he'd stopped her, and then his tight words and unfinished sentences had stopped her again, because pushing through would have meant pushing him too much. And then he'd said it. No retracing old steps, no going back. Just the here and now, focusing on the present. A clean slate, a clear plan, a breathing space…

'Earth to Maddie…'

His eyes snapped back into focus, warm burnished copper with those lighter flecks that had used to seem like stars twinkling when he was smiling. She felt her breath catching low down in her throat. 'Yes. Sorry. What?'

'I was just saying that the windscreen's locked down so you should put your sunglasses on if you don't want bugs in your eyes.' He slipped his own on, then started the engine.

She dropped her shades, heart thumping. The only problem with focusing on the present was that Kaden was very much in it, sitting beside her, stirring memories of a different car, one with a privacy screen and a huge back seat. *Stop!* She needed to focus on something else and fast, something mundane like…the dash. She slid her eyes over it. Black. Dusty. There was a two-way radio with a curly cable dangling, also dusty. She twisted to look at the three rows of seats behind which were higher, to give a better view of the wildlife presumably. The canopy over their heads was beige, tightly sheeted. No windows. No frills. No minibar.

Steve's voice rang out suddenly. 'Hey, Kaden!' He was striding towards them out of the funny little building where she'd gone to freshen up.

'Hi, Steve.' Kaden leaned back, parking a thick, tanned forearm on the door. 'How's it going?'

'Good, thanks. I was just wanting to ask Lina…' His eyes settled on hers. 'Are you okay now?'

Oh, no!

She felt Kaden turning to look at her, could feel his curiosity burning through her skin. The drama of the landing had been so utterly eclipsed by the shock of seeing him again that she'd forgotten all about it. She flicked him a glance, then looked at Steve, feeling heat creeping into her cheeks. 'Yes, I'm fine now, thank you.'

Kaden's attention switched to Steve. 'What are you talking about?'

'Family of wild pigs decided to cut across the runway just as we were touching down. Lina was…'

Pretty please, Steve, don't say freaking out for England!

He licked his lips. 'Lina was concerned.'

'*I'm* concerned!' In one swift movement Kaden twisted back to look at the airstrip, his whole focus seeming to narrow.

'It's all right, Kade.' Steve's voice was placating. 'They got away unscathed.'

'Thank God!' Kaden swung back, the tension in his shoulders visibly melting. His dark lenses met hers for a moment, and then he turned to Steve. 'What's that saying about greased piglets…?'

'I think you mean greased lightening…' Steve was laughing.

She drew in a short breath. So, Kaden was *still* mad about animals, manifestly concerned for their welfare… Made sense. After all, he was here, wasn't he, connected to Masoka in some way. But how exactly? She watched him, the way his hands were juggling the air while he was speaking. That was familiar but there were so many other things to know, twelve years' worth of things that suddenly really mattered, like—her heart pulsed—was he married? Maybe Fran was his wife. *Oh, God!* Fran's emails had always had a vaguely proprietorial tone about them. *We can't wait to welcome you…* And hadn't Kaden used the 'us' word when he'd been talking about her writing the piece? He'd said '*for us.*' Did that mean for him and Fran? And what about kids? Her heart clenched. *Kids!* Was there a brood of little Barrs all freshly scrubbed and lined up waiting to meet her at the lodge?

She looked down at her hands, trying to breathe herself calm. Of course Kaden was married. *Of course.* A gorgeous guy like him was bound to have been snapped up. It was probably the reason why he didn't want to go digging around in the past, because it didn't matter any more. He was shocked to see her, yes, needed to acclimatise, but for him that's as far as it went because he had a life that didn't include her.

She swallowed, letting the thought smooth itself out. If so, it was for the best. It was actually good. *Good.* If Kaden was married, if he had kids, then he must be happy and isn't that what she'd always wanted for him, to have someone who loved him, a person that his family could properly approve of, someone who wasn't a liability—

'So, Lina...' Steve's voice broke into her thoughts. 'I hope you have a good week.' He was backstepping, a smile twitching on his lips. 'Don't let this one feed you to the lions...'

'Shh, *Steve*!' Kaden was stage whispering behind his hand. 'You know I only do that to the *annoying* guests.'

She felt a smile breaking her face apart,

warmth filling her chest. How did Kaden keep managing to make her smile even when she was stumbling around inside her own head? She slid her sunglasses down, looking over the top of them. 'If I make it out alive, Steve, I'll see you next week.'

He threw up a hand, laughing, and then Kaden was revving the engine and they were off, passing the little terminal building, rumbling over a cattle grid, turning onto a dirt road.

Kaden leaned in a little, his voice rising over the engine. 'It's about twenty minutes to the lodge so kick back and enjoy the ride.'

Kick back?

Was he saying that he didn't want to talk? She wound her fingers around her pendant. Whatever *he* wanted, no way she could sit in silence, not when questions were stacking up in her head like Jenga bricks. She flicked him a glance. But how to begin? Which brick to pull out? *So, Kaden, are you married? Is Fran your wife? Do you have kids?* Her chest went tight. No. Personal questions were out, direct ones anyway. It needed to be something more general. Background for the blog piece, maybe. That could work, and if the conversation just happened to spin out...

She shifted, angling herself to face him. 'So,

how come you're here? What's your connection to Masoka?'

His chin lifted. 'I own it.'

'You *own* it?'

He spun the wheel, turning them onto a different, bumpier track. 'Is it such a surprise…?'

Not on his own account, no, but his father had always wanted him to go into the family business and just because Kaden hadn't wanted that didn't necessarily mean he'd have got his own way. But alluding to his father's expectations was probably off-limits because those whispered confidences belonged to the past and they weren't supposed to be going there.

She scanned the *veld*, pale gold, and tangling green stretching to an endless sky. It was Kaden's kind of place, all right. One hundred percent. She took a breath and turned back to him. 'No, actually, it isn't. You always loved wide open spaces and wildlife…' She felt a smile coming. 'Did you do veterinary medicine in the end?'

'Yes.' He seemed to falter and then, perceptibly, he stiffened. 'I got into Edinburgh…'

Edinburgh!

For a beat she couldn't breathe. His first choice. Hers too, for English. She felt a lump thickening in her throat. It's what they'd planned. Being at uni together, living together in some cosy garret on the Royal Mile with a view of Edinburgh Castle. *Stupid!* Everyone knew that the Royal Mile was all short-term lets for tourists, not students, but they'd dreamed it anyway, talked about it, and somehow, God knows how, she must have buried it so deep that it had been nowhere near the front of her mind when she'd asked him about vet school. But now the memory was swelling into the silence like ink on blotting paper, and he was feeling it too, she could tell. It was etched on his face in hard, silent lines.

She clamped her eyes shut, breathing in the smell of dust and sweet grass through the warmth. She couldn't let herself get stuck in this moment. There were things she needed to ask, to know, to protect herself. She couldn't let this silence set hard.

Think!

Maybe… Maybe the way to push through was by simply *pushing through*, pretending she hadn't noticed a thing. Faking it was hardly a stretch. After all, it's what she'd been doing for years, playing a part. She could do this, definitely…

Breathe in. 'Ah… Edinburgh.' *Smile.* 'That's amazing, Kade.' *Draw eyebrows in.* 'Your first choice, wasn't it?'

'Yes.' It sounded curt but then he sighed

and flicked her a glance. 'It was a really good course.'

Relief skipped through her veins. Deadlock broken. 'So, you qualified, and then…?'

'Is this an interview because I haven't exactly prepared.' He looked over, his eyes pinning her over the top of his shades.

'It's not an interview, no, but I do need some background for my writing. I like to get the vibe of a place, understand the people who make it tick…' Was he buying it? Hard to tell, but at least they weren't log-jammed. She shrugged. 'It's just how I work, okay?'

'Right.' He turned back to the road, rubbing a place just north of his eyebrow—a thing he seemed to do now—and then he blew out a breath. 'So…after I qualified, I came out here with Fran.'

Her heart double thumped. 'Fran Palmer?'

'Yes.' His hand fell back to the wheel. 'Fran was on the same course. We were both keen on wildlife conversation, so we came out together, worked as rangers at Kruger for a while, and then somehow we ended up here, at Masoka, working with Richard Petersen…' His expression clouded. 'About a year after we arrived, Richard's health started to fail. We didn't know it then, but he had cancer. He was getting tired a lot, you know, slowing down, so Fran and I took on more and more, helping him to run the place.' His voice cracked into a frown. 'Finally, we managed to persuade him to get a medical. That's when he was diagnosed. Pancreatic cancer. Stage four.'

His jaw clenched, the grief still there. She felt it aching in her own chest. 'I'm so sorry, Kaden.'

He let out a long, ragged breath. 'Richard was a character. Crusty, irascible, stubborn as hell, but underneath he had a huge heart, cared so much about the world. He didn't have any family, just a younger sister in Cape Town who wasn't interested in running a game reserve. He said she'd likely sell it on after he'd gone, that she wouldn't care what happened to it, so he asked me if I wanted to buy it.'

'You mean you *and* Fran…?'

'No.' He shook his head. 'I was the one with the trust fund. *I* bought it.'

A very definitive 'I.' She felt her brows knitting together. So he'd moved out here with Fran, worked with Fran, for, what…years? And yet Fran wasn't part of the financial picture. For all the talking, she was no nearer to knowing what was waiting for her back at the lodge. As for Kaden plundering his trust fund to buy a piece of southern Africa…

She licked her lips. 'It's a lot of land! The

website says it's, what…around six hundred square kilometres?'

'Six hundred and thirty, but actually, it's not enough.' His gaze swung her way. 'There's a parcel of land on the eastern boundary I want to buy.' He shrugged. 'To be honest, it's why we're doing the luxury safari thing, to fund expansion, and to push forward with other projects.'

There it was again, the royal 'we,' but the conversation was tilting in a new direction and all she could do was go with it. 'Other projects such as…?'

'Schools. Clinics. Welfare stuff. Thankfully we don't have a problem with malaria here but there's a lot that's needed, a lot I can help to make better.' A wry smile touched his lips. 'It's funny. You start off thinking about animal conservation, but then you realise that the people here…the economy…' He was shaking his head indulgently. 'It's all meshed so tightly that suddenly you find yourself being sucked into all kinds of community schemes.'

She felt a backwards tug, memories flying in, the way he'd used to rant and rave about animal extinction, man's inhumanity to man, feeling it so deeply, still chewing on it well after everyone else had moved on to lighter fare. And now he was doing something about it, putting his money where his mouth was, expanding his operations into the community, helping others. She felt warmth surging into her chest. 'You do if you're a good person—'

'Steady on.' His glance clipped her. 'I'm making money too.'

She felt a smile coming. 'Kaden, you're making money so you can plough it back in, so there's no point trying to pretend that you're some bad-ass safari tycoon.'

'Some, what...?' And suddenly the boy she'd loved with every fibre of her being was back, laughing into her eyes so hard that his shoulders were shaking. 'Is that even a thing? I mean, I'll bow to your superior knowledge, being the travel queen and all that, but—'

'Travel queen?'

His laughter faded. 'It's what Fran called you...' His gaze drifted frontwards, some new firmness affecting his mouth. 'The queen of the elite travel scene, to be exact.'

'I'll take that...' She felt her own smile slipping, a knot tightening low down in her stomach. Was *this* the moment to ask about Fran? He'd given her a springboard. She might not get another. She moistened her lips. 'I was going to ask about Fran actually. In her last email she said that she'd be the one—'

The two-way blared suddenly, cutting her off.

'Sorry.' Kaden threw her a shrug and un-
hooked the mic. 'Jerry, what's up?'

Typical! Just when she'd got to her big, burning question. Still, it was halfway out now, so
there was no putting it back. She stared at the
speaker, trying to make out what Jerry was
saying but it was all a scramble, or maybe it
was just her nerves scrambling the words. She
bit her lips. Kaden seemed to be understanding everything just fine. He was nodding, and
laughing, talking into the mic, and then he was
looking over, his shades glinting. 'Okay. Okay.
Thanks Jerry.' He slotted the mic back. 'Sorry
about that. Jerry's one of my rangers. He was
just checking in...' He drew an audible breath.
'Anyway, you were asking about Fran...'

'Yes. I was just—'

'She's not here.' He turned back to the road
quickly. 'She left a couple of months ago.'

'Oh...' A momentary relief flared. So, Fran
wasn't his wife. And odds were there'd be no
line of freshly scrubbed offspring waiting at the
lodge either. It had just been her all along, conjuring scenarios, imagining the hardest thing
to bear so she'd be prepared, but what now?
What to say? If only she knew what Fran had
been to him, then she'd know where to put her
feet. She searched his profile, trying to read his
expression. 'I suppose, it *is* a while since her

last email…' His jaw tensed fractionally. Not much to go on! She licked the dryness off her lips. 'I'm sorry I won't get to meet her. We had a good rapport going, you know…'

'Yes, well. I'm sorry too.' He was rubbing his eyebrow again, slowing the vehicle right down so that they were barely trundling towards the next bend. 'The thing is, she wanted me to…' He seemed to be debating with himself, struggling with something. 'She wanted…' He glanced over, and then his hand dropped to his lap. 'She wanted a full partnership and sadly I wasn't in a position to offer that.'

Definitely not what she'd been expecting. Hadn't he already intimated that Fran hadn't had the funds to put into Masoka, that *he'd* been the one with the trust fund? What kind of business partnership could Fran possibly have envisaged? It didn't make sense.

He was pushing up his shades. 'It's been tough because she'd pretty much taken on the whole hospitality side of things, oiling the wheels for the launch, securing *you*, but it is what it is… I've had to involve myself a bit and, in spite of that, it's coming together.' A smile ghosted over his lips. 'I started a new manager last week, Chandapiwa. She's great!' He grinned. 'Very enthusiastic as you'll see for yourself when we get to the lodge.'

She felt a smile coming. Whatever the story was with him and Fran, it was good to see the tension leaving his face, the warmth coming back into his eyes. It was good to see him, full stop!

And then he glanced ahead, and it was more than just warmth in his eyes. It was his entire face lighting up. 'Looks like Jerry was bang on with his intel. Look! We've got company.'

She followed his gaze, and her breath stopped. Barely twenty metres away, a herd of elephants was crossing the road, red dust puffing up around their huge feet as they moved. And then suddenly everything around her seemed to be animating, brightening. She was seeing tall grass rippling, long acacia thorns sparkling with sunshine, rust-coloured termite mounds towering. She could hear a cacophony of chirrups and whistles, could feel the breeze riffling through her hair. All this time, driving with Kaden, she'd barely registered the landscape because of the shock of him, the tangle of him, but now it felt as if the world was coming alive just for her. And the elephants were the icing on the cake. Great lumbering things, smaller ones hurrying behind, wrinkly knees bending, feet almost prancing, trunks going, and then a tiny one came scampering out beside its mother, its head bobbing, trunk scoping the air, its little feet scurrying. She felt her heart filling, tears gathering behind her eyes. 'Oh, my God, Kaden.'

'Isn't it something?' He switched off the engine and sat back, his eyes coming to hers full of light and shine. 'It never grows old, Maddie.'

'I can see that.' She slipped off her sunglasses, suddenly not wanting there to be a barrier between them, wanting only to feel his light warming her face. 'You look like a kid at Christmas.'

'So do you. You look…' The smile in his eyes was softening to a glow, drawing a faster beat from her pulse, pulling at all the old strings, tangling them up all warm and hazy. And then he turned back to the view with a smile in his voice. 'You look as if you've never seen an elephant before.'

She blinked, steadying herself, then refocused on the herd. 'It's probably just that I've never seen one in the wild before.'

'But you're the travel queen! This can't be your first safari…?'

'It is…' She met his gaze, incredulous now, which was easier on the heart than warm and glowing. 'It's just the way things have panned out. I do a lot of spas and island retreats, and exclusive winter resorts. The rest of the time it's city hotels and private villas. The closest

I've come to a safari was a cattle drive I did in Arizona…'

A boyish light filled his gaze. 'Like in that movie, *City Slickers*?'

'No. Think polar opposite.' She felt a familiar playfulness starting. She widened her eyes into his. 'I only do luxury travel remember.'

'So, that's, what—' his lips were twitching '—diamond-studded reins and gold saddles?'

'God, no! Far too hard on the bum. We had well-padded saddles and five-star ranch accommodation. No bed rolls, no beans, no Curly.'

'That's tragic.' He was shaking his head. 'Every cattle drive should have a Curly.'

'We had a Ray.'

'Was he gnarly?'

She felt her belly vibrating. 'Not very.' Kaden's eyes were glowing, and she could feel hers glowing too, and it was so good to be glowing and laughing after all the hedging and the weirdness. She parked her sunglasses on her head. 'Don't get me wrong, Ray knew his stuff, but he was more manicured than gnarly.'

Kaden's eyebrows slid up. 'Manicured?'

She smothered a chuckle. 'He was very nice. Let's just leave it at that.'

Kaden looked pointedly at his hands, grimacing, and then he looked up and his expression altered. 'Uh-oh! Here we go.'

'What?' She followed his gaze, and her breath caught. A huge elephant was coming towards them, ears out, tusks gleaming. Her heart thumped. 'Kade...'

'It's okay.' His eyes came to hers. 'It's just the bull.'

'But you said *uh-oh*, as if it was a bad thing.' The animal was coming nearer, its gait disconcertingly purposeful. 'I mean, what's it doing?'

Kaden's focus was fixed forward. 'He's checking us out.'

'And what does that involve, exactly? Goring...? Trampling...?'

'Only if he's in a bad mood.'

'Is he?'

'I'm not sure yet.'

She flicked him glance. 'How can you be so calm?'

'I'm not.' He looked over, the faintest glimmer of a twinkle in his eye. 'I'm just acting calm for your benefit.'

'Thanks. Way to freak me out by the way.'

'Sorry.'

Impossible!

'Look, what's actually going on here, Kade? Are we in trouble or are you just winding me up?'

'We might be in trouble...' He split a grin. 'Then again, I could be messing with you.'

Like he always used to, except this was an elephant not a tadpole.

And then suddenly he was squaring himself to the wheel, starting the engine. Immediately the animal stopped in its tracks, trunk waving.

'What's it doing now?'

'He's wondering whether tangling with a Land Cruiser is worth a try, so we're going to give him a fright.' His eyes came to hers, serious now. 'Don't be scared, Maddie. I'm going to make some noise, spook him a bit.' A smile touched his lips. 'There will be dust!' And then he was revving the engine, inching them forwards towards the rigid bull, lifting his hands from the wheel. '*Get* on!'

She pressed herself back into the seat, heart pounding. The closer they were getting, the bigger the elephant looked, and it didn't seem to be particularly fazed. But Kaden kept going, taking them nearer, waving and revving, telling the animal to 'Get on,' and then suddenly the bull shrank back, protesting and flapping its ears but backing off all the same, backing down. And then it was turning, hastening off the road and into the bush, leaving a swirl of dust behind. She felt limpness taking over, relief pooling in her lungs.

Kaden blew out a long breath, then turned,

concern flickering behind his gaze. 'Are you okay?'

Time for a little payback. She touched her chest, fanning her face with her other hand. 'Ask me again when I've emptied a bottle of wine.'

'I wouldn't have let him hurt you, Maddie, you know that, right?' His gaze tightened on hers, a protective glimmer just visible that sent a tingle running through her veins. 'Worst case, I'd have got us out of there, but brazening it out was better.'

'Why?'

'Because I can't have the bulls throwing their weight about, challenging vehicles. When we're at capacity, we'll have five Land Cruisers out at any given time. It's essential that our guests feel safe. Aside from any injury or trauma, which would be horrific in itself, an animal incident could bring us a truckload of bad press. It could ruin us.'

'God, I hadn't even thought about danger...' Because even though her pulse was still fluttering, she hadn't felt unsafe for a single second. She'd trusted him completely, had felt safer facing off an elephant with Kaden by her side than she did moving through the regular world where the threats were far more insidious.

'Why would you?' A playful light filtered through his gaze. 'You're just a pampered guest.'

She ran her finger over the dash and turned it over. 'Hardly!'

'Dust is part of the experience.'

'Alongside the mild peril, you mean?'

His eyebrows flashed warmth.

She bit her lips together. This playfulness was lovely, sweet and familiar, but it was starting to feel confusing. She needed to disengage a little, find a different, more neutral track.

She swept a hand through her hair feeling the dust powdering her fingers. 'It's so different seeing elephants like this instead of at the zoo.' She fastened her eyes on his. 'Here, you feel everything, don't you, not just the thrill of seeing them but, jokes aside, also the thrill of your own vulnerability… Does that make sense?'

'Yes.' Something warm and steely came into his eyes. 'One hundred percent.' And then his hand went to the gears, and in the next moment they were moving again, jouncing along the track under an endless blue sky. 'Here you're deep in it, Maddie, feeling all the feels. It gets into your blood.' He smiled over. 'I call it living.'

CHAPTER THREE

HE SHOT MADDIE a covert glance, bracing himself for the little shock that happened every time. Was this whole thing feeling surreal to her too, driving through the *veld* together after twelve years of nothing, seeing off a posturing young bull, bantering back and forth about *City Slickers*? Had to be because it *was* surreal. At least the bantering was familiar, and her smile. That throaty laugh. Better than those questions. Background. Vet school. Edinburgh! Of all the things to have asked but maybe it was just him, being oversensitive.

He felt an ache across his knuckles and loosened his grip on the wheel. Jeez! he was tense. Twitchy. His heart kept missing beats, his breath catching halfway in, or out. It was like being seventeen again except… No… At seventeen he'd been far surer of himself than he was now. Back then he'd been sure of everything. Himself. Her. They'd been joined at the hip, heart and soul. The only thing he'd had to worry about was getting good grades at school. Outside of that, life had been one big party because Maddie was the Tresses girl...

It had been clubbing in all the best places, even though they were underage, and riding in limos, limos with wide seats and drivers who were trained to keep the screen shut and the music on, drivers who'd happily take the long way home for a hefty tip... God, that rich leather smell, Maddie scooting across the seat giggling and kicking off her heels, inching up her tiny dress all the way to her tiny lacy G-string, to that sweet tempting triangle, eyes ablaze, hands seeking him out, stroking, teasing, then very slowly unzipping him—

Stop! Why torment himself? The memories were vivid, but the fact was all those promises they'd made, all that heart and soul stuff, hadn't counted for anything in the end, had it, no matter how real it had felt. Real for him. Evidently not real enough for her! *Oh, God!* And now he was sounding like a petulant, slighted teenager. Thinking wasn't doing him any favours. Time to shift focus.

He took the last bend, pointing the vehicle down the slope towards the river that should have been gushing and roaring but wasn't because the rains were late. Nothing to do with climate change, of course…

'Are we driving over *that*?' Maddie was pushing up her shades, staring at the bridge.

'We are.'

'Is it wide enough?'

He felt his lips twitching. 'Well, it was when I drove over it earlier…'

Momentarily a smile lit her eyes, but then she was looking forwards again, biting her lips. 'Seriously, Kade, you need a wider bridge, with actual sides. This is hairy.'

Fran had thought so too. She'd wanted him to have it widened as part of the upgrade, but he liked it just the way it was, the way it had been in Richard's day.

He touched the accelerator, felt the tyres biting into the planks. 'Maybe so but it means slowing down and when you slow down you see more.' He scanned the riverbank. 'Like there, see…' He flicked her a glance, pointing to the place where hordes of yellow butterflies were congregating in the mud. 'See those butterflies…'

'Ooh.' She rose out of her seat, craning to see. 'What are they doing?'

'Taking in salts and minerals from the mud. That's the theory anyway.' He felt his eyes drifting to her nape, to the little blond wisps curling there, then noticed his thumb moving over his lips. He dropped his hand quickly. 'My theory is that if the bridge was wider, we'd have sailed across without noticing them at all.'

She plonked back down. 'Okay, I concede.' And then she was turning to the riverbank again. 'I'd like to come back and photograph those butterflies. I know safaris are meant to be all about the Big Five, but I like small details, little unexpected things...'

A memory flew in, a tadpole wriggling in his hands, Maddie stumbling backwards into the long grass, shrieking. He held in a smile. 'Well, coming back will be easy. As you're about to see, this place is very close to the lodge.' He drove them off the bridge, accelerating up the steep incline that curved through the trees and onto the wide pale sweep of gravel that fronted the main building.

'Oh, my God!' She was shaking her head. 'You really *are* close to the river!' And then she went quiet for a long moment, taking it in. 'It's beautiful, Kade. Perfect.'

Warmth bloomed in his chest. He could see in her face that she meant it.

He shifted his gaze to the lodge, trying to see it through a first-time lens, but its thick timbers and gently curving thatched roofs were so familiar that all he could see was home, albeit with a few upgrades. The veranda, where he and Richard had used to sit on creaky old chairs drinking sundowners, had been extended, sanded, stained and oiled, and the furniture was all new, square and wicker with wide arms and plump cushions in toning ethnic prints. And there were floor lanterns now, for night-time, and hurricane lanterns dotted about on low coffee tables. It looked inviting. Luxurious. Sophisticated. It was hard to imagine Richard sitting there now.

And then a movement at the entrance brought him back, shooting happy little tingles through him. 'Looks like your welcome party is on its way...'

Maddie turned her head to look at him. 'Welcome party?'

He schooled his voice into a clipped butler tone. 'Of course, Ms. James. I'm only the chauffeur. The real pampering starts now.'

She grinned. 'I like pampering...'

'Good.' He jumped out and went round to open her door. Why was he buzzing? He'd told Fran he wasn't interested in all the frilly bits but suddenly he couldn't wait to show Maddie around. He wanted her to be impressed with Masoka and with his staff—*his family*—and curiously the blog post had nothing to do with it.

He yanked her door open, and no sooner had her feet touched the ground than Precious was coming forward, basket in hand, exactly as they'd rehearsed.

He touched Maddie's elbow. 'Ms James, meet Precious. She's in charge of housekeeping so if you need anything in your suite, just let her know. Precious, this is Ms James.'

The girl's eyes came to his briefly, full of impish light, and then she was smiling, offering the basket to Maddie. 'Hello, ma'am. Hot cloth for you?'

'Thank you.' Maddie took one, unravelling it, lifting it to her face. 'Ooh, it smells lovely. Is it lavender?'

'Yes, ma'am.'

Precious was nailing it, bobbing her head, being supremely courteous. He held in a smile. Behind the masquerade, she was anything but meek. She was deeply mischievous, unswervingly candid.

He shifted his gaze to the man coming forward. 'And this is Tumo. He's going to take your bags to your suite.'

Tumo gave a little nod, smiling. 'Welcome to Masoka Lodge, ma'am.'

'Thank you.' Maddie nodded back. 'I'm very happy to be here.'

'And last but not least—'

'Hello, Ms James.' Chandapiwa rushed forward, radiating joy. 'I'm Chanda, the lodge

manager. You are going to have such a wonderful time with us. We have so much planned
for you.'

'Thank you, Chanda, thank you, everyone.'
Maddie was looking at each of them in turn, her
smile brimming. 'You're making me feel very
special.' And then her eyes flicked to his, lingering for a long, still moment. 'Like a queen,
in fact.'

His heart skipped—*again*—and then it was
filling. She seemed so delighted with everything: the elephants, the butterflies, the lodge,
the staff. It meant she was bound to write a
great piece, so asking her to stay had definitely
been the right thing to do...for Masoka. It was
just himself he was worried about. If she kept
looking at him like this, how on earth was he
going to cope?

'Kaden...' She was dropping her cloth into
Precious's basket. 'Are we going inside now?
I'm dying to see everything!'

'What an incredible room!' She was gliding
through the guest lounge, skirt flaring around
her ankles, one circled with a fine leather thong
that kept drawing his eye. It was hard not to
stare at it, hard not inch upwards in his mind,
conjuring her calves, and knees and thighs. It
was impossible not to remember how those silky

smooth, endless legs had felt wrapped around him, skin to skin…

'Earth to Kaden…'

He blinked and her face came into focus, a mischievous light in her eyes. Could she sense where his thoughts had been, thoughts he shouldn't even have been having?

He smiled. 'I'm sorry, what?'

'I was just saying that your décor is totally on point.' She trailed her fingers over a chair back. 'I adore this tribal print. It's subtle, not over-done.' And then she was moving again, heading over to the grand mahogany sideboard that ran along the gable wall. 'And I *love* this rococo lamp base. It's blingy but in a good way.' She turned, her eyes merry. 'It's an inspired visual disruption!'

He looked at the lamp base. It was hefty, a golden mass of curlicues and flourishes that did somehow work against the plain stone and timber wall. His heart thumped. He hadn't had anything to do with choosing it. It had been Fran, working with the designer, putting in the hours, getting the décor *on point*. He drew an uncomfortable breath, felt his smile vanishing before it had quite arrived. 'I'm glad you like it.'

Maddie's eyes narrowed slightly, and then her gaze shifted. 'Oh, and just look at that fabulous sunset abstract.'

Sunset?

She was walking to the opposite wall, shaking her head. 'It's wonderful...'

His heart thumped again, right up in his throat. It *was* a wonderful painting, a hazy blaze of orange bleeding into a sea of rich browns with splashes of gold and green. Fran had picked that too. She'd said she was going to hang it so it would catch the last of the afternoon light, but it hadn't clicked that the huge smudge was actually a sunset itself. Until now. Until this very moment.

'Is it by a local artist?' Maddie was looking back at him over her shoulder. 'Because if it is, I could mention it in my piece, to give him or her a boost...'

He felt a band tightening around his chest. 'I'm not sure...' Why wasn't he sure? And why hadn't he known that the painting was a sunset? He swallowed hard. 'I could find out.'

From whom, Kaden, Fran?

Maddie was coming nearer, frowning a little. 'That would be great...' She was trying to read him, he could tell, but she was only fuelling the guilt that was suddenly spreading through him like glue.

He broke away from her gaze, looking around the room, *really* looking. Chairs, lamps, art. Ethnic touches. All Fran's work. Each detail lovingly chosen. *Oh, God!* How could he have been so blind? She'd thought she was building a for ever home with him. And he'd been, what, asleep, thinking that the safe, dependable relationship he'd fallen into wouldn't make any demands of him, wouldn't need him to engage more, do more, *be* more? His mouth dried. All this time he'd been cruising, nice steady altitude, no bumps, no bruises, zero likelihood of a sudden vanishing, but he hadn't *seen* Fran, hadn't seen that she was nesting. He felt a drab ache spreading. He hadn't seen her at all outside their mutual passions: the wild, and Masoka. And then she'd spoken, dropped the bomb.

Maddie's voice filtered in. 'But it was just a thought…'

He turned, meeting her gaze, felt his pathetic heart missing for the umpteenth time.

She smiled. 'You know, desirable, not essential.'

She was trying to ease off, but it was too late. He was in tatters.

He forced some words out. 'It's a good thought. I'll look into it.'

'Cool.' Her eyes held him for an interminable moment and then she turned her attention to an art book that was lying on one of the occasional tables. 'Wow! This is nice…'

He swallowed past the dry edge in his mouth.

He hadn't seen Fran, but he was seeing Maddie, all right. The rise of her small breasts under her vest, that luscious bottom lip she was busy chewing, the sweet little blond hairs nestling at her nape. He felt a tug, then a raw, tearing ache. He wanted to plant his lips right into that warm hollow, wanted to breathe her in, lose himself in her the way he'd used to. *Maddie!* She looked so different but the ache building and building inside was the same. He'd never ached for Fran like this, and that must have been a sign, a sign that his feelings weren't right, but he hadn't heeded it. He'd convinced himself that second love wasn't meant to torch your soul, that it was supposed to be calmer, and that calmer was better. He'd told himself it was all fine, but then Fran had laid out what she wanted, and everything had come crashing down. If he could have, he'd have scooped her up and offered her the for ever she wanted, but how could he make himself feel what he wasn't feeling? His stomach roiled. Poor Fran. Did she know how much he hated himself? Had she seen it in his eyes as she'd been leaving? He hated himself so much that he hadn't been able to tell Maddie the truth. He'd tried but the words had got stuck, twisted out into some nonsense about Fran wanting a business partnership. He'd caught the glitch in Maddie's response, but he'd ploughed on.

Ploughing.

It's what he'd been doing for weeks, turning things over and over, trying to figure out why Fran couldn't be enough for him, and now, suddenly, the answer was standing right here.

Maddie...

Gone but still there after all, deep inside.

Maddie...

Bent over the book, all smooth tanned shoulders and graceful arms, pendant swinging, a large drop of amber on a fine gold chain. Had someone given it to her, an old lover or—his breath caught—a current one? He felt his heart shrivelling, taking his gut with it. Why was that such a hard thing to think about, Maddie, with someone else, those legs wrapped around someone else...? He dug his fingertips into his forehead hard. Because he'd wanted to be her last as well as her first. He'd wanted to be her only one. Her everything. Her hero!

That terrible day in her back garden he'd been going out of his mind with it, hammering on the door until finally her mum had drawn him inside, furious, lashing out that Maddie was safe in Paris and that he needed to leave, forget about her. As if! Instead, he'd raced to St Pancras and jumped on the Eurostar, faith firing on all cylinders, believing utterly that love would somehow lead him to her, that if he was where she was, he'd find her. He'd believed it for days, combing those streets, searching, and searching, until his father had appeared and dragged him home.

He closed his eyes for a beat, pushing it all down. That's how much he'd loved her. He'd loved her stupid and now she was here, improbable as a snowflake in June, illuminating the space that Fran had made, the space that Fran had filled with hopes and dreams, and he was drowning in guilt, and yearning, misery and joy, and the worst of it was that she was sensing it, he could tell, mulling it over between the pages of the book. He couldn't stand to watch her slender fingers turning the pages for another second, fingers that had used to trail warm paths over his skin. He needed to go.

He dragged his hands through his hair. 'Maddie, I'm sorry but I've got some stuff to do so I'm going to hand you over to Chandapiwa for the rest of the show-around...'

'Oh.' Her hands stilled and then she looked up, something retreating in her gaze. 'Of course, yes. That's absolutely fine.'

His heart clenched. It wasn't fine. She was hurt. *Damn it!* He wasn't trying to hurt her; he was simply trying to stop his head from exploding.

She lifted her chin a little. 'And you don't have to apologise. I know you must have lots to do all the time…' Her sweet mouth quirked into a not-quite smile. 'Like training the bad elephants…'

His heart clenched again. Now she was trying to make light of it, pretending she was okay when she wasn't. He drew in a slow breath. He'd make it up to her somehow, but right now there was nothing he could do. He needed to be alone, needed to sort out the tangle inside.

He held out his arm, motioning for her to walk, doing his best to sound bright. 'It's not only the elephants, as you'll see tomorrow when you go on your first game drive…'

Chandapiwa was smiling. 'Now remember, if you need anything, just dial one for Reception…'

'Thanks.' She forced out a smile, hoping it didn't look as limp as it felt. What she needed was to be left alone, but even though Chandapiwa was standing tantalisingly close to the door, she seemed not to be in a hurry, any more than she had during the show-around. Through the bar, the dining room, the spa and all around the swimming pool, Chanda had taken her time, talking her through what was on offer, and then she'd strolled her around the numerous verandas that flowed seamlessly around the entire lodge. High ones, built right into the canopy of the trees that crowded the riverbank, some small, for intimate dining, and some that were bigger, furnished with sofas and low tables for taking coffee or enjoying sundowners. The low wide veranda at the front of the lodge, the one she'd seen as she'd arrived, faced out over the golden expanse of the *bushveld*. Chanda had dallied there too, talking about the different species of birds, then showing her the unit where the binoculars were stored, in case she was partial to birdwatching.

Then they'd come along the quiet winding path to her private lodge, Chanda explaining as they walked that Kaden's focus at Masoka was on exclusivity, so he'd spaced out the individual guest lodges, making sure that none of them overlooked each other. *That* kind of privacy was her ideal, and she'd have been lapping it right up if she hadn't been churning away over Kaden's sudden change of mood in the guest lounge.

When Chanda had opened the door and handed her the key card, she'd thought— *hoped*—that she was going to be left to her own devices, but no, the older woman had smilingly insisted on showing her everything: the small kitchen where the private chef would prepare her meals if she decided to use that service, the sitting room with its huge sofa, open fire and a neat mahogany desk—*'for your computer'*—

the luxurious bathroom with its sunken bath and glowing copper fittings and finally the spacious elegant bedroom. All of the rooms opened onto the wide veranda that wrapped around the lodge. Beyond its rustic rails on one side was the *veld*...acacia trees and golden grass stretching into the distance, and on the other side, a cluster of trees with a canopy so dense that it was impossible to see the river below. Now they were back in the entrance lobby.

Chanda's eyes suddenly widened. 'Oh! I almost forgot. We serve afternoon tea on the main veranda at four. If you're not feeling too tired after your journey, you should come, meet our other guests.'

Her heart sank. Making small talk with strangers was the last thing she felt like doing. She mustered a smile. 'It sounds lovely but actually I *am* a little tired.'

'In that case, we'll bring afternoon tea to you!' Chanda beamed, and then finally—*finally*—she was leaving, closing the door softly behind her.

For a moment she stood listening to the older woman's retreating footsteps, and then she blew out a long breath and made for the bedroom, throwing herself onto the vast canopied bed. The pale thatch above was showering sweetness into the air, and she breathed it in, listening to the silence. If only her mind could be as quiet. She'd take that all day long over the drumbeat that wouldn't stop, his name pounding through her head, questions pulsing through her veins. *Kaden, Kaden, Kaden...* Did he really want her here? He'd said he did, but it hadn't felt like it in the guest lounge. All of a sudden, he'd seemed to step inside himself. *Why?* All she'd said was that she loved the sunset painting, and bam! That had been it!

She felt a throb starting in her chest, a hot tingle behind her eyes. Just when everything had seemed to be going well, when they'd been interacting *in the present* as per the plan, having fun even. For pity's sake, what could have been more *in the present* than focusing on the décor, all those gorgeous finishing touches? She'd been in the zone, in work mode, paying attention to the small stuff, because that's the way she rolled. Those small things she pulled into the light added texture to her writing, gave her pieces that extra something that had won her blog so many accolades. She'd been doing *exactly* what Kaden had said he wanted her to do, but for some reason, he'd closed himself off.

She squeezed her eyes shut, bearing down. It had stung. So much. The distance that had vanished while they were watching the elephants and laughing about *City Slickers* had come funnelling back with a vengeance. Thank God for that art book! Page after page, feeling him retreating, feeling tears prickling, because he'd never dropped the shutters down on her before, *ever*! They'd used to fit, hand in glove, but staring down blindly at that book, it had come to her that distance was their biggest part now. And yet, he'd hugged her, hadn't he, and it had felt warm, close, genuine. The opposite of distant. And within moments of meeting hadn't they'd fallen into their old groove, laughing over the Tresses advert? She felt a smile tugging at her lips, tears welling behind her lids. He'd never got that mid-Atlantic accent but hearing him again, hearing him mangling it like before, had felt so good because for a moment she'd been sixteen again, a whole person, a person with a past that went all the way back to an actual beginning.

She bit her lips together hard. How she missed that, sharing a memory with someone who'd known her before, someone she felt safe with. No pretending. No having to be guarded. Nothing short of blissful after years and years of always wondering if the seemingly decent person she was talking to in a hotel lobby or on the deck of a boat was really a journalist sniffing around.

She gulped a ragged breath. The only person she could ever be herself with was Mum, but they didn't talk about the past because her father was stitched through it and neither of them could bear it. But with Kaden, she had a warm hub of memories that were theirs alone. Pristine, untainted memories. Loving, intimate memories. And yes, maybe at first they had been a bit stiff with each other, him not wanting to talk about the past, and her, wound tight over Fran, wondering how Fran fitted, how she'd stopped fitting—that whole *full partnership* thing that still didn't make sense—but in spite of all that, she'd felt the old threads pulling, unravelling, all loose, and easy.

She swept her hands over her face, wiping away her tears. Or maybe she'd only been imagining that warm connection, grasping at old threads because she was lonely, because she'd never found intimacy with anyone else, hadn't even dared to try. Maybe without realising it, she'd latched onto the warmth in Kaden's gaze, latched onto a fanciful notion that he might still have feelings for her, so that when he'd changed, when the light had left his eyes, she'd felt small, and stupid, and stung. She'd tried to hide it, but she'd heard the brittle edge on her own voice. Had he noticed? She got to her feet. Probably not! Too busy moving her along, handing her over to Chandapiwa, making good his escape!

Escape...

She looked at the two holdalls neatly stowed on the luggage rack. Escaping was an option. If Kaden was going to be blowing hot and cold, making her feel like this, then maybe it was the answer. Her stomach knotted. Except it wasn't an answer at all, not when he was counting on her for the blog post. Whatever was jumbling her up inside, leaving Kaden in the lurch wasn't an option. She'd been forced to do it once and wouldn't do it again. *Couldn't!* But being around him was going to be hard. When he was smiling it was impossible not to feel the tug of their old connection, but leaning into it, letting it kindle all the old feelings, was a mistake, a mistake she couldn't afford to make again. No. If she was staying, seeing this thing through for Kaden's sake, then she needed to keep her emotions tied down and not read between lines that weren't even written.

She went to the veranda doors and slid them back, inhaling the warm damp breath of the river. Of course, keeping her emotions tied down was all very well, but she couldn't switch off her brain, couldn't make herself not wonder why Kaden's mood had turned one-eighty when she'd started asking him about the painting. Had she touched a nerve, invoked some hidden provenance? She sighed. That was the problem. Almost everything she knew about Kaden was in their past and twelve years' worth of water had flowed under the bridge since then. Plenty of time for joys and hurts she knew nothing about to have accrued, and now that she was right here where he was instead of a million miles away, she could feel her curiosity itching. She wanted to scratch, wanted to know everything about the man he was now, his hopes and dreams, but what right did she have to ask him anything personal? An ache sawed through her chest. None, because she'd disappeared from his life, hadn't she, decided to sever contact, and yes, she'd had her reasons but looking at things from his point of view, he owed her nothing, least of all his trust. *Oh, God!* How on earth was she going to get through the week?

A sudden bright knock made her jump, then a girl's voice came lilting through the door. 'Tea for you, Ms James.'

She opened up, found Precious standing with a laden tray. 'Shall I take it onto the veranda, ma'am?'

The girl's smile was warm as sunshine and, in spite of herself, she felt her own lips curving up in reply. 'That would be lovely, thank you.'

Precious went ahead, setting the tray on the veranda table, and then her eyes snapped up, a bit mischievous. 'There's a note for you.' She lifted an envelope into view, handing it over with another smile. 'It's from Mr Barr.'

Kaden!

She felt a little wrench inside. Sending each other notes was what they'd used to do at school. It had been a game, sliding notes into each other's bags without the other one knowing, or slipping them, unseen, into one another's lockers. A lump thickened in her throat. This wasn't just a note. It was a message.

'Enjoy your tea, ma'am.' Precious bobbed a little curtsey, a smile still playing on her lips, and then she was disappearing through the French doors. A moment later, the main door thumped shut.

She stared at the envelope in her hands. His writing hadn't changed. She bit her cheek. What was he doing? He'd said he didn't want to revisit the past but what was this if not pulling the past right into the present? Or was she reading too much into it?

For heaven's sake!

She took a deep breath and ripped it open, shaking out the note.

Mads,
Sorry for running out on you earlier. I know it's not what you were expecting. If

you'll have dinner with me tonight, I'll do
my best to explain.
Yours hopefully,
Kaden

She felt her heart buckling, tears wanting to come. So, he *had* been aware of her feelings, *had* heard the torn edge on her voice. And now he was holding out an olive branch. She sucked in a breath. She was taking it, no question, but dinner with Kade in the most romantic setting imaginable was fat-to-fire stuff. She was going to have to keep her head screwed on tight, and her heart tied down!

CHAPTER FOUR

KADEN SHOOK THE ice around in his glass and looked over at the veranda doors. Still no sign of Maddie, but of course he was too early, not by Grandma Barr's five minutes, but by a ridiculous twenty. He downed a mouthful of water, feeling its chill lodging at the base of his throat. *Dope!* Talk about overcompensating. But he hadn't wanted to risk Maddie getting here first and being the one sitting alone in the candlelight, not when he'd been late to the airstrip, then abandoned her halfway through the show-around. This dinner was about smoothing things over, hopefully making things better, not worse.

He slid his eyes over the tall lanterns marking the edges of the deck. Would she like this? Outdoor dining, lamplight, all the sounds of the African night? He lifted his gaze, watching a bat darting and turning. Had she minded him sending the note? He had thought twice about it because it was breaking the rules, invoking the past, but what were the alternatives? Calling her room? Showing up at her lodge door? Either would have put her on the spot, made her feel awkward or, worse, made her feel impelled to say yes to dinner and that was the last thing he wanted. A note had seemed like the gentlest way of asking her without piling on the pressure, so he'd risked it and, miracle of miracles, she'd sent a note back accepting, same loopy writing, same bump to the heart when he saw it.

He set his glass down. The Note Game. Hiding notes for each other to find. Flirty, funny, sexy. Some had been downright dirty. It was why they'd had their burn-after-reading rule, because the thought of her father reading any of that stuff… His stomach coiled. Ironic, all that worrying about Peter discovering that he and Maddie were having sex when the scummy louse had been busy shafting everyone! He ground his jaw. But he didn't want to be thinking about Peter Saint James. Not worth it. It was Maddie he needed to think about, the breathless shock of her, that unexpected realisation that he hadn't let her go after all.

He stared into the lamp flame. He thought he had, thought he'd left her behind, but he must have just pushed her in so deep that he couldn't feel her any more. Not a job of seconds. It had taken years. Years of waiting for something, *anything*, to say that she was thinking of him, that she *loved* him, that she'd be back. After Peter was jailed, he'd thought she'd come back for sure. That was a hopeful time. His belief recharged itself. Belief in *her*, belief in the two of them. He'd thought, no way could she be gone for good, not after everything they'd been to each other, not without a single word. Bright hope attached itself to moments of sunlit hair. He'd chase after her, heart soaring, then have to apologise.

Three years into uni he stopped chasing glimpses and threw himself into pointless sexual encounters that left him empty and aching. Two years on the fantasies stopped: Maddie at the door; Maddie appearing at his table in a café. *Hello, Kaden.* Probably that had something to do with Fran. In their fifth year they did a clinical practice stint together at Edinburgh Zoo. Dark-haired and brown-eyed, petite and blushingly shy, it took a few days for him to discover that behind the careful reserve, Fran was as passionate about wildlife conservation and as hungry for adventure as he was. By the time uni finished they were good friends with a plan in place. Africa. And it was perfect, not only because it offered everything he'd ever wanted professionally, but because it had no Maddie associations.

Until today.

And now here she was, exploding everything, scattering his pieces, making him see things in a new light, things about himself, and about Fran. That awful moment in the guest lounge, guilt rinsing through him like acid rain. He'd had to escape, do his unravelling in private, but he'd carried the look on Maddie's face with him all the way back to his office, that hurt in her eyes, the way her lovely mouth had folded in on itself. He'd never seen hurt in her eyes before, not on account of something he'd done. Pain had never been a part of their landscape, so he *had* to explain, to take the hurt away. That's why he'd sent the note…

But telling Maddie about Fran was a bitter-sweet prospect. It meant opening himself out, talking, leaning into that closeness they'd always shared, and how would that feel? What was it going to do to his poor heart, the heart that on the quiet had seemingly never let her go? *Oh, God!* The coping strategy he'd devised at the airstrip—boxing them into the present—had seemed sound in the moment, but the box was falling apart already.

He slugged back another mouthful of water. Maybe it had been a vain hope all along. He and Maddie had always been talkers, right from that very first moment when she'd put her stiletto through his foot at Rory Fraser-Hamilton's sixteenth. Even the excruciating pain hadn't dented the chemistry. They'd sparked. Crackled. Started talking. God, how they'd talked. Walking—*limping*—and talking and flirting their way through the gardens, and it had felt so easy, so natural. And they'd gone on like that always telling each other everything. Deepest fears. Highest hopes. She'd been his safe house, and she'd said she couldn't talk to anyone the way she could talk to him. They'd kept each other's secrets, secrets like how it weighed on him wanting to be a vet when he knew that his dad had really wanted him to go into the family business, and like how Maddie loved modelling but hated the contempt she attracted from snide hacks who claimed, wrongly, that she'd only got the Tresses gig because she was Peter Saint James's daughter.

He looked down into his glass. And now here he was again, about to let Maddie in so he could clear away the hurt and confusion he'd caused, but it couldn't be two-way traffic. He wasn't ready to ask her about herself or her life, nothing beyond the superficial anyway. He'd only be opening himself up to hearing explanations too painful to bear, or to the possibility of getting attached all over again, and what would be the point of that? She was a rolling stone, here for one week only. He hooked an ice cube out of his glass. Maybe she was in his heart, still, but he needed to lead from the head. He needed to be open and friendly, but also sensible and neutral, like Switzerland.

'Kaden…'

The ice slipped from his fingers. A goddess was gliding through the doors towards him, hair swept up from her forehead, the wide legs of her dark jumpsuit rippling around her ankles.

'Maddie.' He scrambled to his feet, searching his lungs for breath. 'You look—'

'A bit fancy?' Her lovely breaking smile stole his breath again. 'I thought I'd make an effort because I hardly ever get asked out for dinner.'

So there was no boyfriend, no significant other attached to the amber pendant? He felt his heart lifting and contracting at the same time. Who wouldn't want to have dinner with her? She was gorgeous, and clever, and she smelt exotic and orangey, like…what was that shrub Grandma Barr had used to like so much? Philadelphus. That was it. *Stop, idiot.* Why the hell was he thinking about shrubs? He needed to be saying something, something complimentary but also neutral.

He stepped round to pull out her chair. 'I find that hard to believe.'

'Well, it's true.'

For the love of God. Her back was bare, a tempting bow tied at her nape, that sweet, sweet nape. He felt heat pulsing into his groin and gripped the chair back hard, glad that she couldn't see, glad that she was talking away.

'I eat out a lot because I have to write up the food in the places I'm reviewing, but that's work.'

He took a quick breath and tucked her in. 'And this isn't?'

Her face tilted up sharply and instantly his heart froze. He hadn't meant for it to come out like that, implying that she was reading more into this dinner than there was, implying that she was mistakenly seeing it as a date. He was just in a spin because she was dressed to the nines, and she smelt lovely, and he was busy noticing all that when he was supposed to be Switzerland.

He swallowed. 'What I mean is, I'm flattered that you don't consider having dinner with me to be work.'

Her gaze softened a little. 'Well, it never used to be...'

He felt his breath catching low down in his throat. How on earth could he stay neutral when she was looking at him like this, alluding to their old carpet picnics, and everything that had used to follow, because no mistake that's what she was talking about. All he could do was go with it.

He went to take his seat. 'Well, that's because it was usually pizza out of the box.' He aimed a wry nod at the cutlery. 'We're at the grown-up table now.'

'What!' Her mouth stretched and then she was doing the fake double-take thing that had always cracked him up. 'You mean we've got knives *and* forks?'

He chuckled. 'And spoons...'

She screwed her face up into a look of cartoon dismay. 'And here was I thinking that this was going to be a cinch.'

Maddie Madcap! How long would they be able to keep this going? He felt a tug of nostalgia. For ever, because that's what they'd been like, rolling a lame joke along, on and on, until the kissing started. His ribs tightened. But there'd be no kissing now, or ever again. Just talking, explaining.

He laced his fingers together. 'It will be. For you anyway. You were always good with your hands.'

Her eyebrows slid up.

Oh, no. He hadn't meant it like that but now there was no way of recovering without drawing attention to the fact that it had sounded one hundred percent like a double entendre. *Move on!*

He smiled. 'How about a drink?'

'Sounds good.' She glanced at the ice bucket. 'What have you have got chilling?'

'Sauvignon Blanc.' Because she'd always preferred white to red and because champagne would have been too confusing.

'Lovely.' A look came into her eyes. She was onto him, knew that he'd remembered.

He freed the bottle and poured, going slowly to catch his breath. Why was it so hard to stop chinks of the past glinting through? Pizza, and now the wine. Everything seemed freighted, or maybe he was just nervous because of all the Fran stuff, all the explaining he still had to do.

Breathe...

He looked up and his heart boomeranged. The occasion surely demanded a toast, but what?

Lovely to see you?

After twelve silent years.

Here's to us?

What us?

To unexpected reunions?

Because obviously they both relished being thrown into awkward situations like this.

Maybe it was time to pass the buck.

He picked up his glass. 'What shall we drink to?'

'Oh, that's easy.' Her cheeks dimpled into a

heart-stopping smile. 'I think we should drink to this being our very first legal drink together.'

The perfect balance of past and present. She was a genius as well as a goddess.

He touched his glass to hers, feeling a sudden overwhelming rush of warmth. 'To our very first legal drink together.' And then, somehow, more words were coming out. 'It's so good to see you, Maddie...'

A momentary confusion scurried through her gaze and then a warm glow kindled, deepening, holding him fast. 'It's good to see you too, Kade.' She smiled. 'So good.'

His mouth dried. What was he doing? It *was* good to see her—incredibly good—but saying it out loud like that, not just saying it but sounding all wistful about it, was breaching the Swiss border by a million miles. He sipped without tasting, slipped a finger to his collar imagining a tie that wasn't there. That look in her eyes, all warm and deep. He felt sweat prickling along his hairline. But first there'd been confusion, caused by him. He took another sip. Hefty. He couldn't let himself to be like this, confusing her, confusing himself. Whatever happened to leading from the head?

'Nice wine.' Maddie was putting her glass down and then her eyes came to his, her gaze

level now. 'So, anyway, there was something you wanted to say, to explain?'

He felt his heart rate slowing to a treacly bump. The explaining. Exactly the bucket of cold water he needed.

He drew in a slow breath. 'I hear you. You want me to get on with it, right?'

She smiled what she hoped was an encouraging smile. 'I think so.' Otherwise dinner was going to be purgatory. Whatever was on Kaden's mind, he needed to offload it because he was like a cat on a hot tin roof and it was contagious, making her own pulse hop, or maybe her pulse was hopping simply because it was him, *really* him, sitting right there, looking better than heaven.

He put his glass down. 'Okay, first, I want to apologise for bailing on you earlier.' His eyes held her, a gentle light filtering through. 'I know you were upset.'

Her heart contracted. When was the last time she'd heard anyone say *I know you* anything? *I know you* prefer white to red. *I know you* were upset. She felt a burn starting behind her lids. *I know you* were the three words she most dreaded hearing, the words she'd primed herself to kick into the long grass but, coming from Kaden's mouth, they were freighted with

everything, everything they'd ever been, every small thing they'd shared, and it felt like being scoured out and filled up at the same time.

She drew in a breath, trying to sound level. 'I wasn't upset. I was confused, that's all.'

His shoulders lifted slightly. 'Well, either way, I need to explain because it's going to bug me otherwise.' He sighed out a breath. 'Maddie, I couldn't finish showing you around because you were noticing all the things that Fran chose. The textiles. The painting…' He pinched his lips together and she felt a cold weight sinking. He was about to tell her what she already knew, deep down. Those waves of unease coming off him every time he'd mentioned Fran, the business partnership stuff that had sounded so odd, the look on his face when she'd asked him about the painting.

'You're saying that you and Fran were together.'

He nodded slowly. 'Yes.'

She felt a frown coming. 'Why didn't you just say?'

'I don't know…' He shook his head and then suddenly his gaze opened out. 'I think mostly it's because I feel bloody terrible about what happened, and there's no way of explaining it that doesn't make me look bad. And…' Something raw came into his eyes that made her heart

hurt. 'I suppose I didn't want to seem bad to you, not when we'd only just met again.'

She wanted to say that he could never look bad in her eyes, that he didn't have a bad bone in his body, but badness was in the eye of the beholder, wasn't it, and her eyes were still those of a besotted sixteen-year-old. Fran would undoubtedly have a different take on things and without knowing more...

'So, what happened?'

'She wanted us to get married, start a family. Normal stuff, but the moment she said it I realised that I wasn't feeling it. Suddenly I knew that I'd drifted onto the wrong track with Fran.' He blinked, swallowed. 'I wasted her time, Maddie, and the only defence I've got is that I didn't realise...' His voice was cracking, leaking disbelief. 'How lame is that? Wouldn't stand up in court, would it? "Sorry, m'lord. I made a terrible mistake, but you've got to let me off because, you see, I didn't realise."' And then, as if he couldn't bear to hold her gaze, he looked away, staring into the blackness beyond the lanterns.

She felt an ache tearing through. This wasn't Kaden. Kaden had always been in touch with his emotions, known his own mind. He wasn't a drifter, a wrong-road-taker. He knew what passion was, what it felt like, because it's what they'd had together. But she couldn't say that. *Opening old wounds.* She looked at his face, felt her heart flowing out. He wasn't hers any more, but he'd sent her the note asking her to come so he could explain. Maybe as much as anything he needed to offload, talk to someone who knew him well. A friend. She sipped her wine and set her glass down. She could be a friend. It was the least she could do now that she was here.

'What didn't you realise, Kade, that you didn't love her?'

He swung back. 'No, I *did* love her. Just not in the right way, not like—' She held her breath, catching something steely filtering through his gaze, and then he blinked. 'Just not in the right way.' His hands went to his glass, twisting it. 'As I said before, we were uni friends, came out here as friends. It was after Richard died that...' He was shaking his head and then his eyes fastened on hers. 'I can't believe how badly Richard's death affected me, Mads, the stupid things I was feeling, like that he'd abandoned me, as if it was all about me. I mean, God, the poor old stick had terminal cancer! He didn't want to die. He didn't die on purpose, and yet, at his funeral there I was, feeling heartsick, for sure, but also feeling angry.'

Is that how he'd felt when she'd left, heartsick, angry? Easy to imagine all that passion inside him running high, kicking down walls. Had Richard's death dredged it all back up for him or was she misreading herself into his pain?

'I was in a state.' More head shaking. 'I didn't know what to do with myself and then Fran…'

The rest shuttled between them silently. Fran had stepped in, and he'd folded.

He suddenly stopped twisting his glass and picked it up. 'With hindsight, I think that maybe I took Richard's death so hard because he totally got me, one hundred percent.' The anguish in his eyes shaded into a frown. 'You know how I always felt that Dad was disappointed that I wanted to be a vet?'

Was he really reaching back into the past, pulling her along with him when he'd expressly said he didn't want to do that? It was hard to keep up. She lifted her glass, taking a quick sip. 'He was disappointed that you didn't want to go into the family business. It's a different thing.'

He pressed his lips tight and shrugged. 'Maybe, but you know how it used to make me feel, Mads, like I was doing the wrong thing, making some catastrophic career decision?'

'I remember.' Everything had used to run so deep with him, emotions, feelings, even the misguided ones, which is why it was hard to fathom the Fran thing.

'Richard made me feel the opposite, and it wasn't just because we shared the same passion. He made me feel sound, made me feel that what I was doing was right, important!' He took a sip from his glass and set it down, a smile ghosting over his lips. 'It was like he was proud of me, and it meant something, you know. I wasn't looking for a father, but I suppose I came to think of him that way.' His focus drifted and then his gaze sharpened. 'It's why I won't get rid of the old bridge. Richard put it in when he first came here, and I don't want to change it. We've changed so much, adding all these verandas, extending the front so it looks nothing like it did before. Don't get me wrong, I'm pleased with everything, but at the same time it just makes the bridge feel, I don't know, all the more sacred.'

'I get that...' But the conversation was going walkabout. It was hard keeping her place and it didn't help that his eyes were suddenly filling with fond light.

'I'm going on a bit, aren't I?' A corner of his mouth ticked up. 'I know that's what you're thinking.'

Kaden! She felt warmth blooming, a smile arriving. It was such a sweet feeling being *known*, being read by someone who she knew for certain wasn't a threat. She pinched her thumb and index finger at him. 'You are going on just a smidge, but it's okay. Sometimes it's good to let everything out. I think they call it therapy.'

'Therapy!' He chuckled and then his smile faded, but his eyes held on, holding her fast. She felt her pulse gathering. What was he seeing? Was he seeing how much she wanted to talk… about herself, her feelings, just explaining, just letting everything out? He had to be seeing it because she could feel her layers peeling off under his gaze, everything showing through, and she could see something surfacing in his eyes, a small movement on his lips as if he was going to say something, but then suddenly his lips zipped together and he was leaning back in his chair, going for his glass.

'So rewinding to earlier, I suppose what I'm trying to explain is that I fell into a relationship with Fran, and I hurt her, badly.' A moist gleam came into his eyes. 'And then you were looking around, noticing all the things she'd put in place, and it hit me that I must have been sleepwalking all this time because I hadn't noticed any of it, not properly. God, I didn't even know the painting was a sunset, and there you were, seeing it all, asking me about the artist, and all I could think was, how could I have been so blind? How couldn't I have seen that Fran wasn't furnishing the lodge so much as—'

'Making a home?'

'Yes.' He dragged his hands down his face, misery personified. But something didn't feel right. Something didn't fit. He sighed again. 'I didn't think I could feel any worse about Fran than I was feeling already but then seeing your—' he faltered '—your confusion made it ten times worse because I couldn't unpack it all right there and then, couldn't find the words. It's why I had to go, Mads.' He pressed his palm to his forehead, sighing. 'I'm sorry.'

'It's okay.' She tried to load her gaze, so he'd know she really meant it. 'It's not like you planned to have a meltdown, and if it makes you feel any better, Chanda was an excellent deputy.' She felt her lips twitching. 'Her tour was comprehensive and thorough.'

A smile dented his cheeks. 'Talked your ears off, did she?'

'Yep, but in a very informative way.'

'That's Chanda.' He was reaching for the bottle, smiling widely now, looking more relaxed. 'How about a top-up?'

'Good idea.' She watched the wine splashing into her glass.

For all his explaining, the sleepwalking bit still didn't make sense. Hadn't he and Fran ever talked about their feelings, or about the future, not even after their first night together, because that's when everything fell into the light, wasn't it? It's how it had been with them after their first time—the very first time for both of them. She felt a tug inside, an ache ebbing through her veins. They hadn't been able to stop touching, and kissing, looking at each other, saying, *I love you*, over and over again, and oh, how they'd talked, whispering through the night, making plans. Uni in Edinburgh, sharing a cosy garret, picturing themselves together. Naïve probably, but still, if it hadn't felt like that with Fran, then Kaden should have known, and Fran should have known too, because how couldn't she have known that his heart wasn't in it, and if she *had* known and settled anyway, then what had she been thinking? Impossible to know, but it meant that it wasn't all Kaden's fault.

'Earth to Maddie…'

His face came back into focus, his dear face, warm eyes narrowing, slightly quizzical. She felt a pang, something building inside. He'd called himself bad, but he wasn't. He was a good person. Principled. Driven. Fiery. And she'd kept herself away from him, made choices that had seemed right at the time… *Stop.* There wasn't space for that kind of thinking, not now. In this moment, more than anything, she wanted to soften all the blows: her own, Fran's, Richard's. She wanted to make things better, and if that meant spelling it out to him…

She took a breath. 'Can I say something about you and Fran?'

He pushed his lips out. 'Sure.'

'I don't think it's all on you.'

'How?' His eyebrows flickered. 'What do you mean?'

She felt her pulse ramping, drumming in her ears. 'I mean that if two people are together and one of them isn't fully invested, then the other one is going to know it, aren't they, surely…?' She caught something unfolding in his gaze and swallowed past the sudden dryness in her throat. 'I mean, I would…'

His eyes narrowed into hers, and then he looked down, grinding his jaw, his mouth working. 'So you're saying—'

She cut in, suddenly desperate to draw a line under what she'd started. 'I'm saying that if *you* were sleepwalking, then Fran must have been too, so she's as much to blame as you.'

He let out a sharp breath, then seemed to stop breathing altogether. For an endless pulsing moment he stared at the table, and then suddenly his eyes came back to hers, a chink of wry light just visible. He shrugged. 'I don't know if that makes me feel better or worse, but thanks for the insight.'

She felt a held breath trickling out, relief spinning through her veins. He was okay, didn't hate her for meddling. Now she just needed to bring his smile back.

She pressed her lips together. 'You're welcome. Shall I mail you the invoice?'

'Funny!'

But he wasn't laughing. Instead, he was looking at her, his eyes full of comings and goings, and then a familiar glow was kindling, deepening, a glow that in the past would have started a conflagration.

She looked down, tingling, catching the red gleam of her nails and the flowery scent of her own perfume, and suddenly, her stomach clenched. What had she been thinking, getting all dressed up like this, putting on the jumpsuit she'd bought on a whim because it had reminded her of her modelling days, but which she'd never actually worn for fear of attracting the wrong kind of attention? Was it just that she'd wanted to feel like her old glamorous self again, or was it because what she'd said to Kaden before was the God's honest truth: that she *never* got asked out for dinner and she'd wanted to enjoy it, the freedom of being with him, all dressed up on a private veranda, private dining? Or was it that she'd hoped to elicit exactly that glow in his eyes that was now freaking her out? *Gah!* He'd been so right back at the airstrip. They weren't fit for purpose. He was having a Fran crisis, and she was losing the plot, and to top it all she was ravenous.

'Mads…?'

She snatched a breath and looked up.

He was holding menus, his eyes twinkling. 'Since you have it in writing that I promised you dinner as well as an explanation, we should probably take a look at these…'

She felt a smile coming, warmth rushing in. Maybe they weren't fit for purpose, but somehow, they were here, together again, and it was so incredibly good to see him.

Maddie was conducting the air. 'So you've got six guest lodges here, four tented suites at Kgabu Bush Camp, and just the one tented suite at Tlou?'

'That's right…' Her perfume was coming at him in orangey bursts with every wave of her hands. It was distracting, and so were her smooth bare shoulders, but he had his finger on the pulse now. No more breaching borders, no more confusion. He caught her eye. 'Going with low guest numbers works across the board. It means we can charge premium rates for exclusivity and that means more money for expansion, more ranger jobs for the locals and better wages for everyone, all with minimum impact on the wildlife.'

'Sounds like a win-win!' She smiled, then looked ahead. 'I'm assuming you're going for the honeymoon market at Tlou?'

'Absolutely. One hundred percent...' This was nice, walking and talking, sticking to safe subjects. Not that talking about Fran hadn't felt cathartic, but he'd opened up more than he'd meant to, going off on tangents because talking to Maddie had always felt as natural as breathing. Then she'd said that thing about how if he'd been sleepwalking with Fran, it followed that if Fran hadn't twigged, then she must have been sleepwalking too, and suddenly somehow, it had started feeling as if she was trying to remind him of the way they'd been together, holding it up as some sort of gold standard.

That had been hard to take given that she'd left him behind. He'd come close to unravelling, had had to ride it out by pretending to be slow on the uptake, but then she'd made her invoice quip and he'd started unravelling from the other end, remembering how funny she could be, how much he'd loved that about her, how much he'd loved the way she could lighten him with a single quirk of her eyebrow. And maybe she'd read it in him and felt awkward because suddenly she'd been looking away, then he'd felt awkward. Thankfully he'd noticed the menus. Ordering dinner had reset things. Since then, apart from getting himself all steamed up about climate change, he'd managed to keep the conversation rolling on narrow tracks, like this one.

He dodged a noisy, low-flying beetle and looked over. 'At Tlou we're unashamedly milking the whole *Out of Africa* vibe, except there's a luxury shower instead of a water jug.'

'Hang on a minute!' She was giving him the side-eye, mock scowling. 'You can't not provide your honeymooners with a jug. I mean, seriously, *that* scene: Robert Redford washing Meryl's hair, reciting poetry, that blissful look on her face…' She clasped her hands together, clowning a dreamy smile. 'Who wouldn't want to replicate that? I know I would.' And then her smile paled, and she was touching her hair, pulling the short lengths about. 'Not that it would be much of a job these days.'

He felt his heart contracting. Did she miss her long hair? He wanted to know, wanted to know so many things, but he couldn't ask. Oh, she wanted him to, all right. He wasn't blind. No doubt she'd find it cathartic, offloading to him like he'd offloaded to her, but the difference was that he couldn't bear to hear her truths: that she'd thrown him away because she'd stopped loving him, because she'd fallen for someone new in Paris. Because what other reason could she possibly have had for *never* contacting him again after she left? Maybe it was weak of him, but he wasn't up for riding a fresh tide of pain with a grown-up smile strapped to his face, and if she was wondering why he was keeping to his own corner, then it was just too bad.

He looked ahead. But keeping to his own corner didn't make him immune, didn't make him not care. He could still feel her, sense her shadows, same as he always could. The problem was, showing it could cost him more than he had left. He pressed his lips together. But not showing it at all would make him seem cold, which he wasn't. He was the opposite, which was why he was churning away like this. God, there had to be a way through this, surely.

He flicked her a glance. She was walking head down, chewing her lips, little blond hairs sitting sweetly in the hollow of her nape. Such a different look but, actually, it suited her really well, made more of her delicate cheekbones, and it made her eyes seem bigger and bluer. Could she see those things when she looked in the mirror, or could she only see what she'd lost? His heart contracted again. She'd got all dressed up for dinner, and he'd been so busy gawping and gasping that he'd never actually told her how stunning she looked and maybe it was time to do that, let himself off the leash a little bit, so she'd know she wasn't lost on him. He just needed to think of a subtle way in...

He considered for a moment, then nudged her shoulder gently, the way he'd used to when they passed in the corridor at school. 'Hair that's a breeze to wash must be liberating though...'

For a moment she looked surprised and then her shoulders lifted into a little shrug. 'As a matter of fact, it is.' Her fingers went to her pendant. 'I did cry the day I had it cut but it went to charity, you know, for wigs, which meant I got to feel a little bit noble at least.'

'Well done you, for donating it.'

'Oh, lots of people do it.' She was shrugging off his words, but he could see from her face that his approval meant something. 'Anyway, it worked out for the best. I wouldn't want to be toting waist-length hair around now, shampooing it, conditioning it, all that brushing and combing. Such a faff!' Her lips quirked up. 'Unless you've got Robert Redford on standby, of course.'

She was smiling again but it had to be at least partly bravado. Maybe he could fix that.

He took a breath. 'Well, for what it's worth, I think you look great!'

She stopped walking, which meant he had to stop too, and then she was turning, looking up

at him. 'You do? Really?' Tears were mounting at the corners of her eyes. 'You're not just
saying it?'

He felt a pang in his chest. She looked so vul-
nerable, so stupidly grateful. Didn't anyone ever
tell her how lovely she was? Hard to imagine
that, like it was hard to imagine that she never
got asked out for dinner. Still, it left a gap for
him to fill, a chance to balance the books after
forcing her to endure his pathetic ramblings
over dinner.

'Come on, Mads, this is me. You know I
don't just say things. You're stunning—' in for a
penny '—seems that some things never change.'

Her mouth ticked inwards and then suddenly
her gaze was opening out, filling with such a
landscape of light that for a beat he couldn't
breathe. God, she was lovely, maybe even love-
lier than before. Freckles over her nose that he'd
used to kiss one by one, eyes blue as a high
summer sky and those lips, sweet and full, parting softly. He swallowed hard. One small step
would put him close enough to cup her nape
and pull her in. Would it feel like the first time?
Spark. Tug. Searing ache. Would she taste the
same? His belly pulsed. Would she kiss him
back? Her eyes were moving over his face,
going to his lips. He felt a familiar heat rising.
Oh, God, she totally would kiss him back. But

why? What for? Old times' sake? His veins went cold. Enough. He'd drifted onto the wrong track with Fran, and he wasn't letting it happen with Maddie. There was too much at stake. Too much history. Too much hurt. He had to put himself back in his corner right now. *Right now!*

He tore his eyes away from hers and looked along the path, vision pulsing. Her lodge wasn't far. All he had to do was get her to the door, say goodnight and then he could escape, no harm done. He drew in a breath, groping for something to say, but she was already walking, going faster than before. Two strides brought him level with her again.

'Thanks for the compliment, Kaden. It means a lot coming from you.' He felt a shrinking sensation in the pit of his stomach. Whatever she'd detected in him had wounded her and now she was trying to hide it, twisting her face away, rooting in a pocket at her hip. 'What I mean is, apart from Mum, you're the only person I know who's seen me with long and short hair, the only one who can make a comparison.' She produced her key card, then glanced ahead. 'Oh, look! We're here.'

His heart seized. She wasn't meeting his eye, wasn't giving him room to speak. How was this even happening? He'd only been trying to give her a boost and now everything was curdling.

How to fix it? He swallowed hard, looking past her, catching a movement by her lodge door. *Gecko*... The small brown creature was darting up and down, hunting. He felt his pulse tingling, an idea taking shape.

He jerked his head towards it. 'I see your doorman's waiting...'

'What?' She turned, following his gaze, and then suddenly, *miraculously*, she was smiling. 'Ahh, yes. That's James. He keeps an eye on the place for me.'

Relief rinsed through him. Did this mean she was okay, that *they* were okay? He needed to be sure. He ploughed a hand through his hair. 'I'm glad to hear it since that's what I pay him to do.'

'About that...' Her gaze came to his squarely, a trace of mischief behind it. 'He was saying that a pay rise wouldn't go amiss.' She cocked an eyebrow. 'Just passing it on, you know, FYI.'

He felt a smile coming. 'I'll mention it to HR.' She *was* okay. She wouldn't be spinning this out otherwise.

'Anyway.' She was toying with the amber drop between her breasts. 'It was a lovely dinner, Kaden. Thank you.'

'My pleasure.' A kiss on the cheek wouldn't be inappropriate, might even smooth things out more, but if he let himself get that close... No.

Best stay put. He shot her a smile. 'I look forward to reading your review!'

'Oh, it'll be good, don't worry.' Her eyes held him for a long moment and then she was backstepping towards the door. 'I'd better get to bed. Dawn game drive tomorrow, right?'

'That's right.' But not for him. He didn't routinely lead the game drives, but even if he had been scheduled to take her, he'd have swapped with one of the other guides because being around her was too confusing. He waited while she sprang the lock and then he stepped back. 'Sleep well, Maddie.'

CHAPTER FIVE

The pre-dawn wake-up call feels brutal, but a steaming cup of freshly ground coffee softens the blow, as does the smiling face of our knowledgeable guide, Jerry, who's there to greet us when we venture outside...

SHE LICKED HER bottom lip. It was okay. Stoic but upbeat, with a nice bright ring of adventure about it. She attacked the keyboard again...

The game drive information pack—a must-read—advises wearing a warm layer for the dawn outings and it is sound advice. I'm certainly glad of my fleecy top as we clamber into the open vehicle and take off into the chilly darkness...

What to say next? She wiggled her fingers, staring at the screen. She had nothing. Zilch. There was nothing beyond that chilly darkness.

Gah!

She pushed up out of her chair and threw herself onto the sofa. This wasn't *her*. Usually ideas came faster than she could get them down. But now? She pulled her arms over her face, feeling the tightness starting in her chest. The problem was that she was trying to concoct a vibe instead of writing from the heart, writing what she'd actually experienced. But how could she write that Jerry's smile had sent a shock of disappointment hurtling through her synapses because she'd been expecting Kaden to be the one guiding her first game drive. And how could she write that when Jerry had introduced her to her two game drive companions, Birgitte Sommer from the *Cologne News*, and Gerhardus Du Plessis from the *Johannesburg Gazette*, she'd felt a crushing pang of utter dismay.

Stupid Madeleine!

If she'd left off mithering about her father's release for one single second and thought things through when Fran's invitation had landed in her inbox, it would have come to her straight away that Fran was going to be courting journalists alongside the eminent Lina James. Fran was soliciting publicity. She'd had no way of knowing that Lina James was terrified of journalists, that Lina James would sooner chew off her own leg than spend two hours with them jouncing through the *bushveld* in a Land Cruiser!

She'd endured, thrown up the usual defences, keeping herself to herself, obsessing with her camera, but she'd caught the perplexed expression on Jerry's face more than once when he'd turned his bright friendly smile on her, and as for the journos, they must have thought she was seriously weird. She felt her heart contracting. She wasn't weird, she was just scared, scared of being recognised, scared of being challenged about her father, confronted by questions she couldn't answer. The fear was ingrained now, always there. And yet somehow, maybe because of the privacy and tranquillity here, its grip must have come a little loose because that morning she'd felt it tightening back up so hard and fast that she'd almost had an attack.

How had she even got it into her head that Kaden would be guiding the game drive, that it would be just the two of them? It's not as if he'd said it. Last night, he hadn't said, *See you in the morning*, had he? She'd said something like, 'Dawn game drive tomorrow, right?' and he'd said, 'That's right.'

She sat up cross-legged, looking out through the open French doors to the glinting green of the tree canopy beyond the deck. *That's right.* Two words she'd got all wrong. But if she was getting things wrong, getting confused, was it any wonder? Dinner last night had felt like being on a merry-go-round, one moment sinking into pockets that had felt deep and warm and familiar, the next moment rising into an alien landscape of careful conversation. Up and down, round and round, until she was dizzy. And then he'd insisted on walking her back which had seemed sweet and protective, and yes, maybe stupidly she'd leaned into that feeling of being cared for, allowing herself to enjoy the prettily lit path and the warm breeze and the crazy high-pitched trilling of the cicadas, the feeling of him being there right by her side where he'd used to be. It had felt nice. Harmless.

But then they'd started talking about *Out of Africa*, *that* scene, and it had made her think about her hair, and the past, and all the things she'd lost, and she'd felt him sensing it in her like he'd always been able to do. And then he'd said he liked her hair like this, not just said it but said it with that same melting look in his eyes that had always turned her inside out, and she'd felt her heart opening out, a desperate ache starting inside, and for a sublime stretched-out moment it had felt mutual, like something could happen, but then he'd looked away and it had seemed that he was judging the distance to her lodge, as if he couldn't wait to escape. She'd walked on, trying to hide the sting of it, talking away as if she was fine, but she couldn't meet his eye, and then… Then he'd made the door-man joke and she'd remembered that this was Kaden—*Kaden*—who'd never done anything to hurt her, ever.

Her heart clenched. But she'd hurt *him*, hadn't she, disappearing the way she did? Must have. And even if he still found her attractive, even if the desire in his eyes had been real, he'd have quickly remembered what she'd done, wouldn't he? How could he not? No wonder he'd broken the moment to pieces. Kaden was way too smart to put his hand in the fire twice.

She felt tears scalding, a livid heat swelling. It was so bloody unfair. The choices she'd made weren't hers. She'd never have made them if it hadn't been for Daddy. She bit the inside of her cheek hard. *Daddy dearest!* Up to his scummy neck in tar, smothering her in it too, so that it would have rubbed off on everyone and every-thing if she'd let it, especially Kaden and his im-peccable family, pulling them down, tarnishing them by association. That's why she'd stayed away. To save them from that, and—she felt her tears sliding free, trickling down her cheeks—to save herself too, from seeing the open rejec-tion in their eyes, from having to listen to all the polite excuses. Easier removing herself than being removed, than watching their backs turning one by one. Kaden. His family. Her friends.

A sob filled her throat. She hadn't meant to hurt anyone, least of all Kaden, but back at the airstrip, when she'd tried to explain, he'd cut her off, said that he didn't want to get into all that, and she'd got it. In that moment she'd got it one hundred percent. She'd agreed, felt relieved even, but now…

She wiped her face with her hands, then drew up her legs, parking her chin on her knees. Now it wouldn't do. She wanted to explain, had to, so he'd know that hurting him was the last thing she'd ever wanted, and then maybe, once he knew… Her heart bucked. What…? She felt her pulse gathering, drumming in her throat. What was she hoping for? A blissful reunion? A happy ending, now, after all these years? She felt her heart twisting, a cry wanting to come out. *Yes!* It's exactly what she wanted.

Seeing him again, being with him again, was lighting a torch inside, bringing back all the feelings she'd been forced to push down. She'd stayed away because she had to, and then because she'd been too scared to face him, to brave his reaction, but fate had somehow taken that decision for her, and now she was here, seeing that same old glimmer in his eyes, feeling all the old feelings. Now there was a chance to explain, make amends, and if she could do that, then maybe, just maybe, they could start again.

Except...

Her heart pulsed. What if he didn't want to hear her explanations? She swallowed hard. True, last night she'd seen the old warmth coming into his gaze over and over again, and yes, there'd been that brief eternal moment on the path when it had felt like he was going to kiss her, but he had broken the moment, hadn't he? And although he'd said she looked stunning, he hadn't so much as kissed her cheek at the door. And yes, he had opened up about Fran, purportedly because he thought he'd upset her, but he must have known that she'd find out anyway, from Chanda or Precious.

She felt her veins shrinking. And he hadn't asked her a single thing about herself, had he? There'd been ripe moments ready for him to pick, but somehow he'd always seemed to go off on a tangent, monologuing about climate change, the way it was impacting wildlife habitat, and then he'd talked about his plans for expansion, and that had led him onto how Masoka was carbon neutral, aside from the flights required to bring in the clients which he felt bad about but was trying to offset with his community projects, and it had been so good to see his eyes dancing, to see the familiar fire burning inside him that she hadn't minded. But thinking about it now...

She got up and poured herself a glass of water, sipping slowly. Thinking about it now, it all felt rather too deliberate. That feverish light in his eyes, the way he'd never let the conversation stall, filling it up so there was no room for her. Her stomach clenched. Maybe she was getting everything wrong, just like she'd got the wrong idea about the game drive. Maybe Kaden was simply being nice to her because he wanted her to write, what had he called it, *'a cracking piece.'* Her heart froze. Last night, hadn't he even mentioned her reviewing the dinner? She felt a lump thickening in her throat. Oh, it was all falling into place now. He was all about the blog post, wanting to pull in clients so he could do the things he wanted to do. Everything he'd said last night was a sales pitch: emphasising Masoka's green credentials, conjuring the romance of Redford and Streep for the honeymoon bush camp. All things he wanted her to write about. And what had she been doing? Reading too much into the warm moments, reading too much into his gaze, because warmth and desire were what she'd wanted to see.

She felt tears sliding down her cheeks, a fresh well opening up inside. And that was all because she was lonely, so, so lonely. She bit her lips hard, feeling her heart buckling and twisting. She'd tried not to be. She'd tried dating but it had always felt like a minefield. All those questions: Where did you grow up? Where did you go to school? What do your parents do? *Impossible!* She couldn't let anyone in, couldn't trust anyone with her history, never mind her body. Celibacy had been her only option, loneliness the only way she'd been able to keep herself safe, and then she'd landed here, where Kaden was, safe, warm, gorgeous Kaden.

She shuddered out a breath and put her glass down, rubbing the wetness off her face. Kaden was here, and yes, he was all of those things. His smile still made her heart hurt and the glow in his eyes still made her blood sing, but it was time to face facts. He was only interested in the blog post she'd come to write, not her. At dinner he'd said that it was good to see her, and maybe in the moment he'd meant it, or maybe he'd just meant it in a friendly way.

She pushed her fingers through her hair, slow breathing, letting everything settle. That had to be it, because if he'd been interested in her in the old way, he'd totally have taken her on her first ever game drive. If he'd been interested in her in the old way, his curious, smart brain would have got the better of him by now and he'd have been asking questions. She flicked a glance at her watch. Three o'clock! No word from him all day. The writing was on the wall.

She drew in another slow breath. At least she knew the shape of things now. Knowing the shape of things always helped. She went over to the sideboard and picked up the hospitality folder. There was a private chef service on offer, and obviously, Kaden would want her to try it, so that she could write a review! She flipped through and pulled out the menu. Having dinner by herself on her own balcony would kill two birds with one stone. It would save her from accidentally bumping into Birgitte and Gerhardus up at the lodge and it would save her from any more of Kaden's warm, confusing looks across the table, assuming he was even intending to ask her to join him for dinner again!

Kaden struck out along the path, heart thumping. Last night, with the solar lamps glowing through the thick darkness and the scent of Maddie's perfume winding through the air, walking this way had felt very different, except that his heart had been thumping just as hard, maybe even harder. That moment when she'd looked up at him with the past in her eyes. His stomach dipped. He'd come this close to pulling her in for a kiss, but then he'd come to his senses. *Thank God!* If he'd kissed her heaven knows where he'd be now. On the road to heart-ache probably. Not a road he wanted to travel twice.

He strode on, scanning the trees for a flash of avian colour, anything to distract, but there was nothing, just the low afternoon sun spangling through the leaves and the relentless drum-ming in his chest. So much for well-laid plans. He'd intended to keep right out of Maddie's way today so that any lingering confusion about last night had time to fizzle out. He'd checked on the wild dog pups first thing, then checked the state of the watering holes—worryingly dry—then he'd taken a leisurely drive along the east-ern boundary, dropping in on one of the local communities to see how the construction of the new school building he was funding was pro-gressing.

He'd only got back ten minutes ago and the moment he'd set foot in his office, Jerry had ap-peared, minus his usual happy smile. Ms James seemed not to have enjoyed the game drive, he said, and he didn't understand why. They'd seen giraffes, and impala, elephant and rhino, and although she'd been busy with her camera the whole time, she hadn't seemed at all happy. When they'd stopped for coffee and pastries, she'd taken hers to the other side of the vehicle, away from him and the other two guests. He'd gone to make sure she was all right, he said, and she'd smiled at him and said she was fine, but she didn't seem fine. And Jerry was worried that it was something he'd done, or said and, 'Really, Kade, you need to go see her because I don't know what I did wrong. I've never had an unhappy client before…'

And so now, contrary to intention, here he was, heading to her suite with a hammering heart and an ache bouncing between his temples.

Maddie not enjoying the game drive didn't make sense. Her face had been a picture when they'd stopped to watch the elephants on the way back from the airstrip, so how on earth couldn't she have loved seeing rhino, and impala, and giraffes? Unless it really was something Jerry had done or said. *Impossible!* Jerry was a brilliant guide, his best, which is why he'd asked Chanda to put Maddie on Jerry's drive in the first place.

At Maddie's lodge, he went straight to the door and knocked before his nerves could interfere. Within moments there was movement, the sound of feet padding, drawing nearer, and then the door opened and she was there, perfect in a white sleeveless shirt and old jeans, and… that pendant.

'Kaden!' Her eyes lit for an instant and then her face stiffened.

His heart seized. Jerry was right. Something was definitely wrong.

'Hi, Mads.' He swallowed quickly. 'Sorry to spring this on you but can I talk to you for a moment?'

A frown ghosted over her features and then she smiled a smile that didn't quite reach her eyes. 'Of course, yes. Do you want to come in?'

He faltered. Going in hadn't been the plan, but whatever was wrong was beginning to look bigger than a doorstep conversation. He nodded. 'If you don't mind.'

'Why would I mind?' She spun round in one swift movement, heading for the sitting room, trailing a scent of soap and exotic orange.

He snatched a breath and followed, trying— and failing—not to watch the movement of her hips and her cute rear as she walked. Her jeans were old, worn through in places, showing skin. They looked familiar, red tab, button fly. He felt a tingle starting. God, how he'd used to love unbuttoning her, hearing her breath hitch— *Stop!* What was he doing? Those days were gone. Right now, he had a problem to fix.

He forced his gaze into the wider room taking in all her small clues: her phone lying on the open welcome pack; a green garment draped on

the sofa arm; the half-empty jug of water on the sideboard; a pair of sandals abandoned on the rug. Her laptop was on, connected to her camera, and images were flashing onto the screen in quick succession. Jerry said she'd been busy with her camera. Maybe he could start there, break the ice.

He nodded towards it. 'Did you get some good pictures today?'

'Well, I took lots.' She gave a little shrug. 'Whether they're any good or not remains to be seen. I'm just downloading them now. I haven't actually looked yet...' Her fingers went to her pendant, then fell away again. 'I'm sorry, can I get you a drink or something or is it too early?'

He tried a smile. 'It's always five o'clock somewhere right, but no, I won't have anything, thanks.'

'Okay.' Her expression warmed a little and then she bent to pick up a glass from a side table. 'I'm having water.'

'Nice.' He felt a pang in his chest. This wasn't them. Staccato rhythm. Trip-wires. They were smooth flow, nice and easy, or at least they had been. *Don't!* Thinking about the past wasn't going to help. Right now, he had a problem. Maddie was unhappy and he needed to fix that. He swallowed hard, catching her lifting gaze. 'So, not to beat about the bush, I'm here because

Jerry has just told me that you didn't seem to enjoy the game drive this morning.'

'Oh.' For a piece of a second a door seemed to open behind her eyes, and then it closed again. 'Well, it was fine.'

Fine?

'And Jerry was very good.'

Good?

She lifted her chin a little, her gaze edging towards the ceramic. 'You needn't worry, Kaden. I've been writing it up and it'll be favourable.'

As if a good review was the only thing he cared about! He felt a stab of hurt, then a sudden hot lick of anger. He didn't like the cold look she was giving him, and he definitely didn't like the snarky way she'd said his name. He didn't deserve this!

He drew in a careful breath. 'If you've got something to say, just say it. Don't wrap it in a riddle.'

Shock stiffened her face and then suddenly she was blinking, her mouth wobbling, folding in on itself.

His felt his heart collapsing. *Oh, God!* He hadn't meant to upset her. Yes, he was cross, but he thought he'd tamed it well enough, but now, now it looked as if she was about to cry. He took a step towards her. 'Maddie, I'm sorry.'

'No… It's…' She turned her head away sharply, knuckles white around her glass.

A vision flew in, the glass shattering, blood everywhere. He moved in, easing it out of her hands, keeping his voice gentle. 'What's going on, Mads? Tell me so I can fix it.'

She stayed rigid for two interminable seconds and her eyes came to his, wet at the edges, bright with anguish. 'Jerry was right. I didn't enjoy the game drive. I hated every second of it.'

'Why?' What the hell had happened out there? Had Jerry missed something? He licked his lips. 'I don't understand. Jerry said you saw stacks of wildlife.'

'We did. The wildlife wasn't the problem. It was…' She faltered, throat working. 'It was the company.'

'What?'

'Journalists, Kaden.' Her eyes pinned him hard, welling again. 'Of all people, you sent me on a game drive with journalists!'

Journalists! *Of course.* She'd never cared for them, their nastiness, their sideswiping. It's why she'd always used to dive from the nightclub doors straight into the limo on their nights out, because the paparazzi were always waiting.

'How about a picture, Maddie?'

'C'mon, Maddie, strike a pose.'

She'd been sweetly obliging at first but then

she'd found that no picture was ever published without some snide accompanying caption. It's why her mother had sent her away after Peter's arrest, to save her from all that, and worse. And he'd tasted it for himself, hadn't he? Press camped outside his own house and at the school gates, lobbing questions like stones, lenses primed.

'Kaden, where's Maddie?'

'What does she think about her father?'

'Is your family worried about the scandal, Kaden?'

It had meant weeks of slipping out the back, weeks of being driven to school behind tinted glass, weeks of seeing his father tense, tight-lipped.

'Don't say anything, Kaden. We absolutely cannot be associated with that family...'

He inhaled a slow breath, steadying himself. But it was a long time ago, water under the bridge. Except—he brought Maddie's face back into focus—maybe it wasn't, for her. His heart thumped. She'd changed her appearance because of the media, but she was still blonde, still cropped, wasn't she? And what about her blog? His ribs went tight. When Fran had shown it to him it had struck him as odd that there was no smiling picture of Lina James, only oblique fragments indicating a presence: a hand around a lens; a pair of feet in the sand; a skewed reflection in a bistro window. He'd taken it for artiness but now?

He ran his eyes over her face. Sweet lips pinched tight, something hollow behind the steel in her eyes. His heart thumped again, pieces starting to fit. Those mirror shades that hadn't seemed like her kind of thing. Short hair. Fake name. Faceless blog. He searched her gaze. Was she still scared, even now, still hiding, after all this time? *Oh, Maddie.* He felt his heart opening, flowing out towards her. He could keep her safe, shield her...

Stop.

What was he doing, firing up the old noble instincts? There was no role here for his inner hero. The cold hard truth was that if Maddie had ever wanted him to save her, protect her, she'd have reached out a long time ago.

He broke away from her gaze and went to put her glass down. Even so, it wasn't healthy for her to be living under a perpetual cloud of paranoia. Twelve years on, who the hell was going to be interested? That juice was well and truly extracted. Could he at least help her see it, help her get past it? He felt his stomaching dipping. It would be ideal if he could, given the circumstances...

He turned back to face her. 'Look, Maddie

I'm really sorry that you didn't enjoy the game drive. I know that journalists aren't your favourite people, but the thing is, I didn't *send* you out with them because I was being insensitive. It's just that, well, the way Fran pulled things together...' He felt his stomach tightening. This news was going to go down like a lead balloon. 'The fact of the matter is that all of our guests this week are journalists.'

'What?' Her face bleached. 'All of them?'

'Yes, but they're travel writers, not gossip columnists. They're not paparazzi.' He went to stand in front of her so he could measure the effect of his words. 'They're interested in good food, and lovely views, and spa treatments. That's what they're paid to write about, that's what they're focusing on.'

Her gaze was locked on, listening, but it was still loud, still panicked. Why? It didn't make sense. These people weren't a threat, except to him maybe... He felt a tingle. Now there was an idea, a way to take the weight onto his own shoulders so that hers could feel lighter. It was worth a try. He took a breath, venturing a smile. 'If you think about it, it's me who should be worrying. If Masoka doesn't pass muster, then I've got a huge problem.'

Her face softened a little. 'Masoka more than passes muster, as well you know.'

'Thanks for the vote of confidence but until the reviews are in…' He shrugged, catching a glimmer of warmth in her eyes, but behind it the shadows were still there.

He rubbed his eyebrow. What else could he do? What more could he say, except more of the same? He fastened his eyes on hers, loading his voice with everything. 'Look, seriously, these journalists aren't a threat. Not to you. Surely you can see it?'

A wet gleam was filling her eyes again, and suddenly he couldn't stand it, couldn't not touch her. He took her shoulders into his hands. Maybe he could pump faith into her somehow through his palms, bring the light back with one last ditch attempt. 'Do you remember the story of the Japanese soldier who stayed in the jungle for years and years because he didn't know the war had ended?' She was blinking, opening her mouth to speak, but he couldn't let her interrupt. He had to finish, *had* to free her. 'Can't you see? The war's over. You can come out of the jungle.'

Her heart gave. Kaden's gaze was so warm. So earnest. So achingly dear and familiar. And that touch… She could feel her shoulders throbbing around his hands, awareness tingling though her veins. How long was it since she'd felt the warmth of a hand on her shoulder, let alone two? How long since she'd bathed in such clear light? Copper light, flecked with concern, copper light intent on putting her mind at rest, and it had nothing to do with reviews and write-ups, she could see it now. *Oh, God!* How could she have even thought that? She'd wound herself tight for nothing because she was always on the defensive, primed for slight. But this was Kaden. *Kaden!* Who'd never hurt her, ever!

'Jerry has just told me...' And he'd come straight away, hadn't he, to make sure she was all right. No note. No calling ahead. Just there at the door, breathless, as if he'd been hurrying. Warmth came surging into her chest. The writing was on the wall. On some level he must still care but he wasn't up to speed, didn't understand the whole situation.

She felt her ribs tightening. She'd wanted to talk to him, hadn't she, wanted to open up, but starting with this...? She felt a cold weight sinking. This was the place where her dread lived. Right now, his gaze was loaded with kindness, but would disdain filter in when he knew? Would he step back, rub his head in that new way he did? Her heart thumped a heavy beat. Whatever, there was no avoiding it now, witnessing his reaction. She inhaled, willing her lungs to keep working. Maybe it was for the best, facing it, finally. At least she'd know the shape of things.

She put her hands over his, squeezing them for a moment so he'd know she appreciated his warmth, and then she lifted them away from her shoulders. 'The war isn't over.'

His gaze sharpened. 'What do you mean?'

Her throat closed over. Why was this so hard? She was innocent. Why couldn't she seem to throw off the weight of this shame? *Come on, Madeleine.* She swallowed hard, trying to keep her voice level. 'Dad's getting out.'

A frown flitted across his face, but there was no disdain, no sudden detachment. That was something.

She pushed on. 'It's happening this week. I don't know the exact day.'

'Okay.' He pressed his lips tight and shrugged. 'I suppose it had to happen sooner or later…' And then suddenly panic flared in his eyes. 'God, I'm sorry. I'm assuming you don't, but maybe you do…' His eyes were reaching in, narrowing. 'Do you see him, visit? Are you…? Do you still—?'

'No!' She could feel bile rising into her throat. How could he even imagine that she had any affection for her father? She locked her eyes on his. 'I hate him, Kade. You've no idea how much. No. Idea.' She could feel her neck prickling, the back of her nose, her eyelids, a torrent starting. 'He was supposed to do good in the world! He was supposed to be a good man!' She could hear her voice cracking, breaking in two. 'He was supposed to love me, but instead he stole my life!'

'Oh, Maddie.' He was shaking his head, his gaze softening into hers, and then suddenly his arms were around her, pulling her close, and it felt like falling over a finish line, collapsing to the ground with euphoria pounding. She felt a sob coming, expanding with all the hate inside. It was too much, this sweet, sweet feeling of being held against him warm and tight. *This* was what she'd lost, exactly *this*, and feeling it again was hurting, hurting so much that it was almost unbearable, but the thought of moving was unbearable too because he was stroking her hair, talking softly. 'Shh. It's all right. It's all right.'

She screwed her eyes shut, pressing her face into his shirt, feeling her tears seeping out, seeping, and seeping. 'It isn't though.'

His hand stilled. 'Look, your dad's getting out. So what? Who cares? He's a footnote.'

If only!

She dragged in a breath, wiping her face, easing herself out of his arms. 'He isn't a footnote. He's headline news.'

'How?' Kaden's eyes were suddenly wary. 'Why?'

'Because he's written a memoir.' Kaden's face stiffened, his gaze cooling. Was this the nail in the coffin for him, the bridge too far? She felt her gorge rising, a sudden pang of nausea. Might as well finish. She swallowed hard. 'It's coming out this week, to coincide with his release.'

Silence. And then…

'You have *got* to be joking!' Kaden was turning circles, dragging his hands through his hair, and then suddenly his eyes locked back on, blazing. 'I mean, seriously, Mads, who the hell's going to buy it?'

She felt her soul shrivelling, her voice shrinking. 'Everyone. It's already a bestseller, prerelease.'

'God almighty!' His throat was working as if he couldn't get enough air and then he exploded. 'The world's gone mad! The planet's burning, habitats are being destroyed, animal species are being wiped out, and people are putting money into the pockets of an utter shitbag like your father! People actually want to read what he has to say…like it could possibly count for anything?'

She closed her eyes. Bad enough hearing it inside her own head all the time but hearing Kaden blasting it out was somehow making it worse. 'I know.' She pressed her fingers into her eyes, trying to staunch a fresh spill of tears. 'You've no idea how proud I am to be his daughter.'

'Oh, Madeleine.' Kaden's hands slapped to his sides, his voice suddenly softening into gentleness. 'I'm so, so sorry.'

She looked at him. Kindness in his eyes. Sorrow. Empathy. Her heart lifted. He didn't despise her. She was still here, still standing, wilting a little admittedly, but it was over. Telling him about her father had been an ordeal but she was on the other side of it now, seeing warmth coming into his eyes, not distaste.

He sighed a deep sigh. 'So I get it now, why you found the game drive so tough.' He shrugged. 'For what it's worth, I still think you're safe here, but...' He paused, seeming to weigh a thought, then he carried on. 'But if you're going to be uncomfortable around the other journalists, then I feel duty bound to offer an alternative arrangement...' There was a smile hiding at the corners of his mouth, a spark of mischief gaining ground in his gaze that was giving her tingles.

'What kind of alternative arrangement?'

His eyes crinkled. 'It's more of a one-to-one service, really. Very exclusive, although the drive guide's a bit of a maverick.'

Her heart skipped. 'You mean *you*?'

He nodded, breaking into a smile. 'I'm not nearly as good as Jerry but I'm at your service for the rest of the week if you want me?' His eyebrows flashed. 'What do you reckon?'

Was he mad? How could she not want him?

She felt a smile flying through her veins, exploding in her cheeks. 'Honestly, I reckon it's the best offer I've had all day.'

CHAPTER SIX

'THEY'RE ADORABLE, KADE...' Maddie was watching the wild dog pups through the long lens of her camera, elbows propped on the Land Cruiser door. Her voice was low, mindful of their proximity to the animals, but there was excitement in it. Delight.

He smiled inside. Delight was good. Watching her now, glowing the way she'd used to, it was hard to believe that just yesterday she'd been vibrating with pain and anger and hate. She was cut so deep, courtesy of her scumbag father, but the worst of it was that the depth of her pain had shocked him, and it shouldn't have. He felt guilt curling, flaking off into his veins. It absolutely shouldn't have because he knew how much she'd loved Peter, how proud she'd been of him.

He rubbed his eyebrow. It had seemed to cost her so much to tell him about Peter's release and about the book. Why? None of it was her fault.

It wasn't like him, with Fran. Guilt was the reason he hadn't come clean to Maddie about Fran straight away, but the book thing, he just didn't get. Then again, had he ever really tried to *get* Maddie's situation, ever truly let his imagination roam into her reality? He licked his bottom lip. No. He'd been too self-absorbed, hadn't he, too ensnared in his own hurt and loss to think about how it must have felt *being* her. Somehow, in his bruised juvenile mind, she'd always been the one with agency, the one who'd spirited herself away to a life she was happy to lead—without him—but then being fair to himself, what was he supposed to have thought because the fact was, even if leaving hadn't been her choice, she'd never come back, had she? She'd left him dangling, hurting, wondering. Had she ever stretched her imagination to that, to *his*, reality?

Stop! Why was he tangling himself up like this? The only reality that counted was this one, the present, this soft dawn moment in the *veld*, Maddie clicking away on her camera, smiling all the way to her cheeks. This was a moment worth staying in.

He lengthened his gaze to the dogs. 'They *are* adorable. I love watching them.'

One of the pups stilled, sniffing the air, and Maddie pressed the shutter. 'It's so sad that most of them will die.' She looked over. 'Aren't you ever tempted to do something?'

'Er… *Hello?* I think running a game reserve counts as doing something.'

Her eyebrows flickered. 'Well, yes, obviously, there's that.' She turned back to her camera. 'I just meant that aren't you ever tempted to, you know, save one, take it home?'

'At the level of the heart, yes, but that would be meddling, and mankind's done quite enough—'

Wait a minute. Her shoulders were shaking and there was something very suspicious about the way she was pulling the camera closer to her face. Was she teasing him, provoking one of his ranting monologues to see how long he'd go on before realising?

He felt a playful spark igniting, a smile loosening in his cheeks. 'Very funny, Ms James.'

Dancing eyes flicked to his, wicked, glinting.

His pulse jumped. Her body language was one hundred percent invitation. He could feel his fingers itching. Did he dare? *Hell, yes!* He lunged at her, going for her ticklish spot, and she exploded, giggling hard, twisting away from him, camera up.

'Pax! Pax! Mind the camera. Kaden, *mind* the camera!'

She was panting, her body a warm curve,

smooth shoulders turned, vest straps slipping, gold chain against her golden nape, that sweet hollow. He felt heat pulsing, a vibration starting in his belly. 'You should have thought about that before.'

Her body curled tighter. 'No, Kade. No.' But she was giggling, eyeing him over her shoulder, beaming out another challenge.

He went in again, laughing, catching her on the turn, pursuing her just enough to generate another fit of giggling, but then suddenly she was twisting back sharply to face him, lips parted, breath coming in short bursts.

'Listen.' Wide eyes gripped his, blue as cornflowers. 'Let me go. We're disturbing the pups.'

'Listen... Dad's coming... Can't you hear him...? Kade, I'm serious! Let me go.'

Which had never meant let her go at all. It had meant the opposite, adding a frisson of danger, heightening the tension, stretching out that sweet moment of surrender. And he could feel it now, danger thrumming, the thrill of the tangle, the warm scent of her filling his nostrils, a blur closing in at the edge of his vision, closing in so that all he could see was her face, her eyes, her lips—

'Listen!' Her voice jerked him back and then he heard it, the high-pitched rippling chatter of the dogs, the excited whining and squealing. She was wriggling, impatient now. 'What's going on?'

He blinked. What *was* going on? What was he doing? He released her, heart pounding, lifting his gaze to the commotion at the den. 'The hunters are back. You should watch.'

'Oh, look at their tails going.' Her voice was husky, breaking a little. 'They look so happy to see each other.'

'They are.' Patchiness in his own voice too. 'They're family.' He swallowed hard. Had that tantalising closeness really just happened? Had he gone too far? It didn't feel like it. It had felt like old times, her teasing, him diving. He flicked her a glance. She seemed fine, settling back behind her camera. But why had she started it?

He felt his stomach roiling, then shrinking. What was happening here? What was he getting himself into? He'd offered to be her guide for the week because she'd been crying in his arms, warm and soft and broken, and he couldn't stand her pain. All he'd been thinking...all he'd wanted, was to give her some peace of mind, save her from having to worry about the other journalists, but what about his own peace of mind? Suddenly that peace was feeling very fragile. Was spending time with her like this a good idea? Barely two hours into the day and he was already falling off the wagon, succumbing. His heart clenched. The problem was how not to when every smile, every teasing glance, made his skin start to beat.

Fran had never used to make his pulse race and tumble like this. Petite, brunette, hardworking, Fran was a serious type, not given to teasing. She was like him. It's why he'd related to her, why they became friends. *Why they'd plodded along.* But there was no plodding with Maddie. It wasn't only that she was still the best thing he'd ever seen, it was that he liked her, and he liked the person he was when he was with her. They'd used to be so good together, comfortable enough to be wild, comfortable enough to be open. Not being open was an effort, not asking things was an effort, things like where she'd got her pendant, why it was always there around her neck. So many questions all leading to the biggest, scariest one of all: why she hadn't come back to him.

His ribs went tight. He wasn't ready for that one. And he was going to have to stop himself from falling into rose-tinted alleys as well, because rose-tinted alleys led to tickling, and tickling led to confusion, and God help him, wasn't he confused enough already?

'Ugh! Gross!'

Maddie's voice snapped him back. She was

rearing away from her camera, grimacing. He switched focus to the pack. *Ah!* No wonder she was grimacing. The hunters were regurgitating red gobbets of meat onto the ground. It wasn't the prettiest sight, but it meant they'd made a kill.

He met her eye, holding in a chuckle. No one grimaced quite like she did. 'Look, they have to bring it back somehow. They don't have shopping baskets.'

'Pity, because *that* would be a great picture, whereas this—' she waved her hand towards the pack '—is definitely not luxury travel blog material.' She settled the camera on her lap and then she looked up. 'So, while they're busy doing the hoofing-up thing, maybe you can tell me all about them...'

There was that glimmer of mischief again. More teasing, but he wasn't falling for it this time. 'That could be a very long monologue and I know how much you enjoy those.'

She smiled an acknowledging smile and then a soft light came into her gaze. 'Okay, so instead, tell me why you love the dogs so much.'

'Is it that obvious?'

'It is to me.'

To me. Was she deliberately invoking their old connection or was he getting paranoid?

'You couldn't wait to get here, and you were smiling all the way. You're like a proud father.'

She had him, although the dogs weren't the only reason why he'd been smiling all the way here.

His heart pulsed. That thought had slid in on the sly, hadn't it? Smiling because of the pups, and—*admit it*—because of her, because he liked being with her, because setting off into the pale dawn with her had felt amazing.

He licked his lips. 'I am a proud father. And I think I love the wild dogs because they know how to live.' He could feel his blood stirring, the passion rising. 'They help each other, Mads. They look after each other. The dogs we saw with the pups at the start aren't the parents. They're babysitters.' He flicked a glance at the pack. 'If you look now, you'll see that the baby-sitters get a share of the kill, even though they weren't on the hunt.'

She turned to watch, then her eyes came back to his, glowing. 'That's wonderful.'

'It is.' He felt a familiar grey pall descending. 'In many respects I think that wild dogs are better than humans. Humans don't share any more, they just take.'

A shadow flitted across her face.

Oh, God! Way to put his foot right in it! He hadn't been thinking of her father, just humans in general. He swallowed quickly. 'Hey, here are some factoids for your blog. Each animal has its own unique coat pattern, and, unlike other dogs, they only have four toes.'

'Four toes?' Her eyes narrowed a little and then a slow smile curved on her lips. 'You once told me that you only had four toes.'

What? And then it came rushing back. 'You remember that?'

Something flickered behind her gaze. 'Yes, I remember.'

Unbelievable. Just two days ago he'd been thinking about it as well, not the part about toes, but about Rory Fraser-Hamilton's sixteenth, colliding with Maddie. *Falling hook, line and sinker.* He felt his mouth drying. Sharing the memory would be opening a box, and she knew it. That's why she was looking at him so carefully. He felt his pulse gathering. Did he want to open that box? Did he have a choice? Because if he didn't, it would be tantamount to stonewalling her, and that would spoil the mood, the day, everything. He inhaled a slow breath. What harm could it do? It had been fourteen years ago. Just two kids at a party. One of them with only four toes. Apparently.

He licked his lips. 'I didn't say that. You're not remembering it right.'

Her eyebrows ticked up. 'I think I am...'

He felt a smile straining at his cheeks. 'No. What happened was that we were dancing with our different friend groups, then you twirled, lost your balance and put your stiletto through my big toe.'

Her mouth froze. 'That's a gross exaggeration.'

He dipped his chin at her. 'And—' this was fun, watching her eyebrows climbing to maximum elevation '—then you said you were sorry, and I said, *"It's fine, I can walk with four toes—"*'

'*"But my dancing days are over!"*' She was laughing, clapping her hands together softly. 'You're right. That's exactly what happened. And then we went outside...'

'To see if I could still walk...'

'Which you could, but then it was me, remember, struggling on the gravel path because of my shoes...'

The dusk closing in, pipistrelles darting above the darkening trees, the pink remnants of the sunset clinging to the horizon, the circular fountain plashing white water, the beat of the music thumping across the wide sweep of lawn and *her*, hair longer than the dress she had on, and those ridiculous, lethal shoes. It was locked in.

He nodded. 'I do. You took them off at the fountain and got in.'

'Not just me. You did too.'

Because he hadn't wanted to be even an inch away.

Her eyes were filling with dismay. 'Your poor toe. Black and blue. I felt so bad.'

He pressed his lips tight. 'To be honest it's never been the same.' He winced for effect. 'It still twinges sometimes.'

Her eyes narrowed into his. 'Very funny!'

He felt warmth blooming in his chest. That had been fun, and not scary at all, but it would probably be a good idea to quit while he was ahead.

He shot her a smile, going for the ignition. 'Right, I think it's time to find a suitable place for breakfast.'

'Here we are.' Kaden switched off the engine.

It wasn't the most inspiring breakfast spot. A flat hardpan, bald save for a few small boulders and sparse tufts of pale green grass. Where the dust ran out, a low monotony of scrubby acacia started, interrupted only by the occasional stricken remains of a dead tree. In the far distance, hazy in the early morning light, low hills rose, similarly clad in low green scrub.

She shot him a glance. If it weren't for him—hearing him laugh, feeling the warmth coming through his smile—she'd have been feeling a little disappointed, but as it was, she was fine.

Simply being with him was enough. A joy. *And* they were talking, peeling corners off memories, having fun. So much fun. Crazy how simply being herself, her real self, could be so intoxicating. No one watching, no one overhearing, no burdensome sleazeball of a father weighing her down. This was freedom—living—and even if Kaden's perfect breakfast spot looked a bit like an empty car park, it was still a slice of heaven, a slice of heaven that, for some reason, he was scrutinising with great care.

She caught his eye. 'What are you looking for?'

'Buffalo.' His gaze moved on again, combing the terrain. 'They're unpredictable, AKA dangerous.' He motioned right. 'About five hundred metres that way there's a river—more of a trickle right now because the rains are late—but it's a draw, which means there could be buffalo about. I'm not letting you out of the vehicle until I'm sure we're alone.'

Now the choice of location made sense. No animal would be able break cover without them seeing it. She felt a little rush of warmth. He was keeping her safe, protecting her, and yes, thinking about it, Jerry had parked in a similar spot yesterday, a dust bowl with clear views all around, so obviously it was standard practice, but still, something about the way Kaden was being so intensely forensic was making her feel special.

'Right!' He turned finally. 'We're good to get out, but no wandering off, okay?'

'Like I'd even consider it now that you've thumped the buffalo drum.' And then suddenly, because he was looking so serious, it was impossible to resist a little mischief. She looked at the scrub and frowned a nice deep frown. 'In fact, actually, I think maybe I'll stay right here.'

His eyes narrowed momentarily and then he nodded. 'Okay.'

She pressed her lips together, willing herself not to crack. He was on the hook, settling himself in for the game just like he'd used to, that mirthful spark just visible in his eyes.

He opened his door. 'Sadly there's no in-vehicle steward service but obviously it's up to you. If you'd rather stay here while I sit on the fender stuffing my face, then it's absolutely your call.' He dipped his chin, giving her a long look that contained the tangible gleam of victory. 'After all, at Masoka, what the guest wants the guest gets.'

She felt her belly vibrating, laughter spilling out. 'Oh, you're good.'

His eyebrows flashed—up, down...up, down.

'Stop it.' He was too funny, too breathtakingly handsome. 'I'm conceding, okay? You win.'

'Yes!' He punched the air and then he was chuckling, pinning her with an irresistible copper gaze. 'Who's the daddy?'

She felt her breath catching. 'That would be you.'

His eyes held on for an endless second and then he was moving, jumping out. 'Coffee, madam?'

'Sounds good.' She cracked her door, heart drumming. Had that felt like a moment because it *was* a moment, or was she just high on life, high on Kaden essence? Whatever, she was tingling all over, feeling giddy. Was he?

She slithered out, going round. 'Is it the same great coffee Jerry had?'

'It is.' He'd already got enamel mugs and a picnic box set out on the folding bumper grid and he was busy pouring. 'Do you still take milk?'

A pang caught her in the chest. She'd given up milky coffee in Paris. The small bitter espressos had felt like a better fit for her bitter black moods, but she didn't want to get into that with him. Not now. Yes, they were talking, breaching some walls, but rushing fences when they were still finding their feet didn't seem like a good idea.

She smiled. 'You remember.'

'Not the hardest thing.' He put a steaming

mug into her hands. 'We spent a lot of time at Book Stop...'

...after school, at their special table on the mezzanine. The bookshop café had always been quieter than the mainstream places, and warmer, with that nice new-book smell. They'd sometimes started on homework, but mostly they'd held hands, whispering and flirting and, when no was looking, kissing.

'Croissant?' He was holding out a box, a smile hanging on his lips.

The pastries smelt divine, looked authentic. She wanted to say so but that would only lead her to back to Paris. Into the dark.

'Thanks.' She took one and turned to look across the *veld*. So empty and yet the air was alive with squawks and whistles and clicks. The word *teeming* came to mind. That was how it felt here—that you were just one creature among many, no more important than the rest but alive to the tips of your senses. What had Kaden said?

'Here you're deep in it, Maddie, feeling all the feels. It gets into your blood.'

Her spine quivered. He was right. She was feeling all the feels, a strange and wonderful elation stirring, because of this place and—she turned back to him—because of him. The combination of Kaden and this place was close to overwhelming.

'You okay?' He was rubbing crumbs off his hands. 'More of anything? Coffee?'

She lifted up her mug and croissant. 'I'm still going, thanks.'

'Slowcoach.' His eyes crinkled and then he turned to freshen his own cup.

She felt the hairs on her arms standing to attention. He looked so good. Irresistibly tousle haired. Irresistible full stop. His blue shirt was laundered soft, the sleeves rolled up, showing tanned forearms that had never used to be so thick. He'd grown into his man's skin, filled out in all the right places, but his hips were still slim and, if the contours inside the seat of his cargos were anything to go by, his tush was still firm as an apple. She felt a low-down ache starting. Hot. Tugging. Raw. Yesterday, crying in his arms, it had felt as if there was still something warm and real between them. The way he'd stroked her hair, so gently, like she was a precious thing, the way it had felt so right, so perfect...

But torturing herself with fanciful notions was foolish. He might have been warm, yes, and sweet, but the wall of the past was still there, the past he didn't want to revisit. Maybe, by degrees, bits were crumbling off but the memories they were sharing were safe ones: Rory's party, Book Stop. They'd still been kids then. Fourteen and fifteen. They hadn't made their promises yet, hadn't made love yet. Recalling those things was a world away from the messy part, the going-to-Paris part, and the afterwards part, the hard-to-explain part when insecurity had taken her prisoner. A knot balled tight in her stomach. Would they ever get to that and, if they did, would anything she said make sense, because, increasingly, all the things she'd thought were beginning to seem incomprehensible even to her.

She bit her lips together. But she couldn't think about that now. She needed to stay in this moment, keep things rolling along all light and airy. Neutral. Also, she needed to be thinking about the blog piece at least a little bit.

She finished her croissant and swallowed a mouthful of coffee. 'So, Kade, what are we actually hearing? I mean, I can't see anything but there's all this noise.'

'What are we hearing?' His head tilted, listening, and then suddenly he was levering himself up onto the hood, holding out his hand. 'Come sit and I'll tell you.'

That face. Those eyes. Setting off shivers.

She parked her cup on the bumper and put her hand into his. Warm. Dry. Familiar. Strong! The bonnet felt warm too, and there was his arm, so close that she could feel heat radiating through his shirtsleeve. She flicked him a glance. Was he feeling it, this tingling awareness? If he was, he was hiding it well. He seemed intent on the business of listening.

His eyes clipped her suddenly. 'So, this one—' a low, grating vibration was starting, getting louder and more raucous '—is guinea fowl.' He scoured the *veld* and then his hand shot out, pointing. 'There! See…'

She caught a low hastening movement in the long grass close to the scrub line. 'Yes. I see them.' Plump and black, white-spotted. Vaguely comical. She felt a smile coming. 'I like those.'

'They're ubiquitous.' He leaned away a little, smiling into her eyes. 'It's adorable that you're so thrilled.'

Her heart skipped. 'Ubiquitous doesn't stop them from being appealing.'

'True.' His gaze held her for another sweet moment and then he turned back to the view. 'The constant trilling sound is cicada, and *this*…' His finger went up as a *tock* sound rose into the air, then repeated, going faster, escalating into a sort of a hiccup: *tock-tock, tock-tock, tock-tock*. His teeth caught on his lip. 'That's the southern yellow-billed hornbill, otherwise known as the flying banana.' He leaned forward, combing the landscape. 'If I can just locate it…' And then his hand shot out again, pointing. 'On the bare branch over there…'

She followed his gaze. 'Yes, I see it!' A biggish bird, with a pale grey breast, black mottled wings and huge yellow beak that did look exactly like a banana. 'He's rather handsome. I should get my camera.'

'Will you get a good enough shot from here?' He was shifting back, the swell of his arm pressing against hers.

Warm. Firm. Heavenly. Suddenly the thought of moving was beyond unappealing. She looked at him. 'You've got a point. Closer would be better.'

Which had an unfortunate ring of double entendre to it, or maybe it was just her.

He smiled. 'I'll keep an eye out when we head off. We're bound to catch one close to the track at some point.' His eyes held hers for a long still moment and then they narrowed a little. 'I'm curious. What's with the pendant? You're holding on to it as if it's a lifeline.'

Her heart clenched. She *was* holding it, hadn't even noticed, and now he was asking, and it was Paris again, erupting, inescapable. Paris. So close to the raw spot, so close to all the hurt. But he didn't know that, did he? He was looking at her, his eyes all warm and curious. No hidden layers. *Oh, God!* He had no idea he was pushing them into the messy part. Her heart was drumming now, thumping in her throat and in her ears. Maybe talking about it would be a good thing but were they ready? Her mouth dried. No. But lying about the pendant wasn't an option. She'd never lied to Kaden, and she wasn't about to start.

She drew in a breath, then leant to pick up her cup from the bumper. 'That's because it *is* a lifeline, kind of...' She took a quick sip, then met his gaze. 'It was given to me by a friend of Mum's... Renée Colbert...' She swallowed hard. 'In Paris...'

A dark light flickered through his gaze.

'Paris is...' Her throat was thumping hard. 'Paris is where I went when Dad was arrested.'

He seemed to falter, and then he blinked. 'I know.'

'What?' Her heart pulsed. This couldn't be right, surely, and yet his eyes weren't lying. She searched her mouth for moisture. 'How?'

'Your mum told me.'

Mum...

'When?' Mum had never said anything about any such conversation with Kaden.

'The day your dad got arrested. You weren't at school. You weren't answering your phone, so I went to your house. I wanted to see you...' His eyes flickered. 'Didn't she tell you?'

'No. She never said a word.' Not then, not since.

His mouth tightened. 'That figures.'

'How?' Nothing was figuring. Nothing was making sense. 'Please, tell me, what happened?'

He gave a little shrug. 'It was lunchbreak. When I got to your house the press was camped outside so I went round the back and over the wall.'

Ten feet high and planted with a dense yew hedge on the garden side. How on earth had he even done that?

'I knew your mum was inside, but I had to bang on door for ages before she finally opened up. She told me to leave. She was distraught, obviously, but I wanted to know where you were.' He was shaking his head. 'I wouldn't go. I was loud, and stubborn, and then she got angry, exasperated. She said that you were safe in Paris and that for everyone's sake I should go back to school and forget about you.'

Her heart seized. And he'd have gone back to school, of course, but he hadn't forgotten her, had he? He knew she took milk in coffee—or had—and he remembered Rory Fraser-Hamilton's party, and Book Stop, and the stupid Tresses catchphrase. Why hadn't Mum said anything?

She looked into his face. Remnants were glistening in his eyes, tugging at her heart, but what was worth saying now? As for Mum… She felt her fingers tightening around her cup. Maybe it was just as he said: Mum not telling her figured. Knowing he'd been at the house ranting and raving would only have made her cry harder, miss him more. Mum wouldn't have wanted to inflict that on her. And anyway, Mum had had her hands full, playing dutiful wife to the scumbag, keeping her famous daughter safe. To Mum, her teenage romance with Kaden must have seemed like a trivial sideshow next to her husband's scandalous extravaganza. And later, when she might have mentioned it, she'd probably decided that it wasn't worth rattling loose, not when Lina James was all moved on, making a success of things. No. She bit her lips together. There was no one to blame here, except her father. *Daddy!* Only him.

She drew Kaden back into focus, feeling warmth surging into her chest. 'I don't know what to say except…thank you.'

He shrugged. 'For what?'

'For scaling a wall. Breaching a yew hedge. For caring about where I was.'

His eyes clouded, then turned steely. 'Did you think I wouldn't?'

She felt a pang inside. 'No, of course not…' The doubts had crept in afterwards, hadn't they, the fear taking root, growing firm and strong, pushing out everything else. But telling him that when he was looking at her like this was impossible. Rather, he needed to hear something good from her, something equal, so he'd know that she'd been confounded too.

She tipped the dregs of her coffee into the dirt, then fastened her eyes on his. 'When they came for Dad, Mum confiscated my phone. That's why you couldn't reach me, but in any case, she'd made me promise not to contact friends, or the agency, and especially not you.' He was opening his mouth to speak but she knew the question that was coming. 'She was worried about my phone being hacked. She was worried about your family being associated, being brought down in some way through us.'

A shadow lengthened behind his eyes, and then he nodded an acknowledgement.

She felt relief unwinding, tears prickling. His understanding meant the world. 'Mum was so strong, Kade. She had all Dad's crap to cope with, but she was set on protecting me, set on limiting the damage. I had no choice. I had to do what she said, even though I didn't want to, because I knew that whatever I was feeling, however stunned, and angry, and heartbroken I was, it was a million times worse for her.'

'I'm sure.' His eyebrows flickered and then his gaze shifted past her, disappearing to some inner place.

I'm sure.

She put her cup down. What did that mean? It seemed inadequate, somehow, but then again, what was she expecting? *It must have been awful for you all, Maddie. I understand completely. Of course you had to disappear. And it's fine that you didn't message, or call, ever. I'm cool with that.*

Her heart thumped a dull beat. He was rigid. Staring at nothing. So close and yet so far. She felt her insides twisting. What a mess. What a total, utter mess. Her heart thumped, then missed. She could feel absence expanding, her throat starting to close.

Oh, no.

The familiar darkness was coming, threading through her veins, drawing the tightness in. She gasped, trying to breathe, trying to stay calm, but the spots were starting, dancing before her eyes, and her lungs were locking.

Please no.

She went for the pendant, gripping it hard, pushing back.

Focus! Smooth. Smooth. Smooth. You are alive. You are here. You are fine.

She went to swallow but her throat wouldn't work.

Come on! Breathe! Breathe!

'Hey...' A warm hand closed around her arm. 'Are you okay?'

Kaden's eyes swam into focus, wide, full of concern, then blurred.

Breathe!

'Maddie...' His voice was low, urgent, bending towards panic.

Her heart jarred. She couldn't have him panicking too. It was bad enough that she was having an attack. She dragged in air through her nose, felt her lungs sticking, then opening, taking it in, letting it out, settling, everything settling, heart, pulse, head, stars. She swallowed, breathing. Just breathing. The cicadas were trilling again, and Kaden's eyes were reaching in, and there was a delicious sensation of warm fingers at her nape, stroking, sending tingles shooting through her veins.

You are alive. You are here. You are fine.

'Maddie?' Copper light, blazing. 'Maddie, talk to me.'

She blinked, swallowing again. 'I'm fine.'

'Are you?'

His head was so close to hers she could feel his hair tickling.

'Yes.' She inhaled again, pushing air into every recess. 'It just happens sometimes.'

'Panic attack?'

'Yes.' It felt so good, letting it out. 'It's what I was about to tell you about the pendant—'

'Being a lifeline?' His fingers stilled for a beat and then they were travelling downwards from her nape, palming slow lulling circles.

'Yes…' She could feel her focus sliding, her eyes wanting to close. 'The attacks started coming after I moved to Paris. At first, I didn't know what was happening. I'd be out walking or sitting in a café and then suddenly I'd be gasping for air, paralysed, terrified. It got that I was too scared to go out.' Renée's face filtered in, kind, careworn. 'Then one day Renée came home with the pendant. She said I should try to use it as an anchor.'

Kaden let her arm go and took the amber drop into his hand, weighing it. 'It's certainly hefty.'

She felt a smile coming. 'It needs to be. It has to do a lot of work. When I start feeling out of whack, if I can make it my centre, then it pulls me back.'

'So if I see you grappling for this, then I should pay attention?'

His hand was so close to her breasts that she

could feel its heat, could feel her nipples responding.

'Yes. No.' *Focus.* 'Not always. Not now. I think a lot of the time I touch it because it's there. I hardly know I'm doing it.'

He smiled. 'Well, just in case, I'm going to be keeping my eye on you.' He released it gently, and then he was on the move, vaulting off the hood.

She watched him packing away their cups. *Kaden...* He'd scaled a ridiculously high wall and battled through a yew hedge in his school uniform just to see her. He'd been meticulous about checking for danger before allowing her out of the vehicle, and now he was on panic attack watch. And he hadn't seemed to care about her dad's release, or about his stupid book either, at least not in any way that related to her personally. Her heart contracted. He was the same, the same as he'd always been. Noble, kind, passionate. Perfect.

She felt a burn starting behind her lids and turned away, staring across the *veld*. Had she got everything wrong, built herself a jungle to hide in, staying away when all this time—she felt a sob filling her chest—all this time she could have been by his side, giving him love, being loved—

'Maddie!' The urgency in his voice spun her

around. He was in the vehicle holding the two-way, his face bleached. 'A bull elephant just charged Jerry's vehicle. No one's hurt, thank God, but I've got to get back right now.'

'Oh, my God!' The sob in her chest died, adrenalin taking over. She scrambled down and ran round to the passenger seat, clambering in. 'What are you going to do?'

'I'm going to find the elephant.' He started the engine and then they were pulling away fast. 'Posturing is one thing, like the bull we encountered, but this seems to have been spontaneous aggression. Unprovoked. It points to the animal being in pain.'

She gripped the door top hard as he threw the vehicle round a bend. 'But how are you going to find it?'

'The rangers have got the drones up already. By the time we get back, hopefully they'll have got the location down.'

She scanned the *veld*. Expansive, dense with acacia. The dust trails weren't exactly autobahns but at least the going was clear. Driving through the vegetation would surely be far too arduous. She licked the dust off her lips. 'And then what? I mean, how are you going to get to it?'

'In the chopper.'

She felt her eyebrows shooting up. 'You've got a chopper?'

'Of course.' A smile lit his eyes momentarily. 'It's essential out here, the only way to get anywhere quickly. Mostly, I use it for veterinary work.' They slewed around another bend stirring dust. 'So, once I know where this elephant is, I'll dart it from the helicopter, then examine it. With a bit of luck, I'll find something wrong, something I can fix.'

'But you'll have someone with you, right?' She was thinking of the buffalo, how careful he'd been before he'd let her out of the vehicle. In the thick of the *bushveld*, there could be all kinds of danger lurking: buffalo, lions, leopards. Stinging things, biting things. *Snakes!*

'Step away from the pendant, Mads.'

She felt it between her fingers and let it go quickly.

He was laughing, his eyes pouring out copper light. 'I always go with a team. You don't have to worry.'

Easier said than done. It was great that he was so well set up for getting to the elephant and treating it, but even so, she was going to be counting the seconds till he got back.

CHAPTER SEVEN

'WELL, WELL, WELL. If it isn't the flying vet!' Maddie was smiling, looking fresh and completely lovely in a long brown skirt and vest. 'I heard you found the elephant. Did it go okay?'

'Yes.' He felt a smile coming, partly because of the elephant, but mostly because the sparkle in her eyes was contagious.

'So don't just stand there. Come in.' Her hand was on his arm, tugging gently. 'I want to hear all about it.'

His pulse quivered. Just her hand but the contact was sending lightning bolts through his veins. *Again.* He'd felt them that morning too when she'd been trying to escape his tickling fingers, and again when she'd been sitting next to him on the hood of the Land Cruiser, her warmth seeping through his shirtsleeve. Unforgivably perhaps, he'd even felt a tingle when she'd been having her panic attack, well, not during the actual attack itself—at that point he'd been on the verge of panicking too—but just after, when she'd been calming down, and he'd been stroking that sweet spot at the back of her neck. Truth was, he couldn't stop tingling around her. Never could.

He stepped inside, following her into the sitting room. Same exotic orange scent trailing in her wake as last time, but this time he wasn't dropping in unannounced. This time he was invited. Her note had been waiting for him when he got back. Dinner at her lodge, courtesy of the private chef, an excellent service, she'd said, which he really ought to try for himself. He wasn't going to argue.

'So what would you like to drink?' She was opening the doors of the minibar, giggling a little. 'As you can see, I have everything.'

'Or do you mean you've *had* everything?' He felt a smile tugging at his lips. 'You seem sort of high.'

Her eyes caught his. 'I am high, but it's got nothing to do with alcohol.' And then her expression changed, growing serious. 'I'm just glad you're back, that's all, in one piece.'

He felt his breath going still. The pendant in her fingers as they'd been driving back.

'But you'll have someone with you, right?'

That drop of amber wasn't only a focal point she used to pull herself back from the edge. It was a tell, the thing she touched whenever she was unsure of herself. She was touching it now, lightly. His heart thumped. Because she was telling him, in a roundabout way, that she cared about him, and it was making her nervous. And yet if she still cared, then why had she left him high and dry? He got that her mother had taken her phone away, got why she'd made Maddie promise not to contact him. With the wisdom of maturity, he could understand all that, but what he didn't understand, still, was why she'd stayed away. He felt his stomach tightening. Why had she done that if she cared? He wanted to know, wanted to ask, but Kristopher was coming in, his chef's whites almost as dazzling as his smile.

'Good evening, Mr Barr. Ms James.'

'Good evening, Kristopher.' Was there a second, secret smile going on behind Kristopher's eyes? It felt like it.

Kristopher's gaze shifted to Maddie. 'Just checking that you still want—'

'Yes! Absolutely.' There was a firmness in Maddie's tone, a smile hiding at the corners of her mouth. 'Everything we agreed before, okay?'

Kristopher flicked him a glance, then nodded to Maddie. 'Very good.'

'And we're going to be having a drink first, so we'll be ready to eat in about twenty minutes…' Her eyes came to his. 'Or longer? What do you think?'

'I'm easy.' He could feel a chuckle sitting high in his chest in spite of the thing he wanted to ask. There was something irresistible about the mood in the room, something that was lifting him, carrying him along like a tide. 'Whatever you're cooking up and whenever you want to eat it is fine by me. It's your show.'

Her cheeks filled with a smile. 'Okay.' She turned back to the chef. 'We'll go with twenty minutes.'

Kristopher nodded and then he was turning, disappearing through the door.

'Now, drinks.' Maddie was launching herself at the bar again. 'I'm having a G & T.'

'I'll have the same.' Not his usual drink, but suddenly appealing after the all the dust and grit of the day.

He watched her pouring and mixing, the nimble movements of her smooth, toned arms. She was graceful, effortlessly elegant in her understated outfit. Beautiful. And also suddenly, somehow, right in front of him.

'Here.' She put a clinking glass into his hand, then lifted her own. 'Cheers.'

'Cheers.' He touched his glass to hers. 'First legal gin and tonic—'

'Or...' Her eyes lit. 'We could toast the elephant?'

He felt his lips twitching. 'I think the poor elephant has had a tough enough day already.'

She chuckled. 'You're on form tonight.' She took a sip, then set her glass down, stepping back a little. 'So, tell me all about it.'

'*All* about it?' He felt a smile rising inside. 'Are you sure?'

Her chin lifted. 'Absolutely.'

'All right.' He sipped, taking the moment to enjoy the anticipation in her eyes. 'So, when I got there, the bull was clearly agitated but I couldn't see any obvious injury, so I darted him, and then I found the problem.

'Which was?'

'An abscess on the underside of his dominant tusk. Fortunately, it wasn't huge, but it was dripping pus and—'

'Eugh!'

Right on cue! No one grimaced quite like Maddie. It was why it was so much fun to tease her. He pushed down the smile that was jumping like a flame inside and shrugged a fake apology. 'Sorry! I'll spare you the gory details.' He lifted his glass to his lips, not drinking. 'You don't want to hear about the lancing...and the draining...and the irrigating...' Her head was tilting, her eyes beaming out a warning. He felt his smile breaking free. 'And you especially don't want to hear the details of how we medicate...' She was coming towards him now, narrowing her eyes into his, a smile curving at the corners of her mouth. He felt a gleeful spark exploding inside. 'How we have to clear out the rectum so we can shove a handful of antibiotic paste inside.'

She stopped in her tracks. 'You've had your hand up an elephant's bottom?'

'Not only my hand.' He couldn't hold in his laughter, couldn't resist miming the action. 'It's more of a whole arm action, to get the antibiotic right up there.'

'All that way?' She recoiled ever so slightly. 'Sheesh! You had a glove on, right?'

'It's more like a wader for the arm.'

Her eyes darted to his shirtsleeve. 'Very noble.'

She was cracking him up. 'Maddie, this is a different shirt, and yes, I have showered.'

She flicked him a mischievous smile. 'That's a relief!' And then her expression softened. 'Seriously though, I think you *are* noble. I'm so impressed with what you're achieving here. You're doing what you always wanted to do, helping animals, working in conservation. It must feel so good.'

The naked admiration in her eyes was touching. He felt its warmth reaching inside, filling him up. 'It does, but then writing an award-winning travel blog must feel pretty good too.'

Her eyes flickered, registering the compliment. 'It has its moments, although nothing that comes close to, you know...' She grimaced, mimicking him with the antibiotic, and then she shrugged a little. 'Compared to yours my life is rather trivial.'

He felt a pang in his chest. Is that what she really thought? He searched her gaze, trying to see behind it, but she broke free suddenly, folding her arms.

'Anyway, what's the prognosis, doctor?'

She was moving him along, but he couldn't stop his wheels spinning. How could she think her life was trivial? He didn't understand everything, but the fact was she'd had her life ripped away and she'd built another, one that by any standards was a success, in spite of her father and in spite of her fears and her panic attacks. She was stronger than she knew. More determined, more wonderful—

'Kaden.' Her voice broke in. 'Will the elephant be all right?'

He collected himself. 'It should be. We'll keep an eye on him.' He took a sip from his glass and set it down. 'I'll probably have to knock him out again in a week or so to give him a check-up, but he certainly seemed much calmer when we left, and calm is good.' He felt a cold weight shifting. 'Calm doesn't upset travel writers.'

'Oh, my God!' She was blinking. 'Can you believe that I of all people had forgotten about the journalists? Are they okay?'

He swallowed hard, trying to ignore the queasiness that was making a home in his stomach. 'One of them was fine. She has experience of game drives. She said she knows this kind of thing can happen.' His stomach roiled. 'The other one was a little less stoic.'

'Meaning?'

Concern in her eyes, tinged with faint alarm. His stomach clenched. Why had he even mentioned it? Because he was quietly freaking out, because he'd wanted to tell someone who got him, someone who knew that the last thing he'd ever do was play fast and loose with the safety of his guests. But it was a bad move. Selfish. He couldn't finish, couldn't tell her about the reception he'd got from Gerhardus Du Plessis. It would only feed her phobias, and besides, he was probably reading too much into it. Of course Du Plessis had been shaken. Of course he'd needed to vent, and who better to vent at than the actual owner of the game reserve? In the heat of the moment that was what people did. God, it was not as if he was a stranger to a spot of venting himself. And Du Plessis was bound to have calmed down by now because that's also what people did. Hell, through the haze of a champagne glow, he might even be finding some perspective, coming to view the whole incident as a bit of an adventure, something to dine out on.

He inhaled carefully. It was all going to be fine. Not worth worrying himself about, and definitely not worth worrying Maddie about, not when she was looking at him like this, her fingers busy again with that damn pendant. He was going to have to bat away fast, make light of it, for her sake.

He arched his eyebrows in the way that had always used to make her smile. '*Meaning* that I'm down one magnum of Dom Pérignon.'

'Ahh!' Her lips pressed together. 'Do you think it'll work?'

He felt a dull ache starting at the base of his skull. Right now, he didn't care if the sweetener worked or not and he definitely didn't want to devote another second to thinking about it or talking about it because it was killing the buzz. He wanted to see Maddie happy and smiling again, not taking on his woes. She obviously had some sort of surprise planned and *that* was the important thing, the only thing that mattered. How was he going to get them back into that happy zone? And then he knew.

He pressed his lips together. 'Who knows if it'll work?' He made a show of walking towards the door. 'I'm way more interested to know what's going on in the kitchen.'

Quick as a flash, she blocked him, her eyes glinting. 'Oh, no, you don't!'

He felt laughter percolating. Way to restore the buzz.

He arched his eyebrows. 'Oh, yes, I do.' He faked left, went right, but instantly her hands were around his arm, holding him back.

'I *said*, no, you don't.' She was giving him a laser stare, tightening her grip.

He stilled, staring back, feeling his breaths coming short and quick. In a few moments the light in her eyes would change. Trust would filter in and then—

'I'm not letting you go.' Her gaze was gleeful, unswerving. 'I see you, Kaden Barr. I know what you're up to. But I'm older now.' One eyebrow slid up. 'Wiser.'

The pressure of her fingers increased and suddenly the lightning bolts were back, taking off, crackling through his veins, sending heat pulsing into his groin. *Oh, no.* He was getting hard, very obviously hard. But he couldn't make himself move. It was too tantalising, being tethered to this moment, feeling time stretching, everything slowing down, funnelling into this space, this aching, blissful space. Was she feeling it too, the lightning, the pulsing, the wanting? Yes. Oh, yes. He could see it starting, just like old times, that haziness coming into her eyes, the small silent movements of her mouth, her lips parting—

'Ms James.'

The two words hung in the air, dangling on and on, and then somehow—*somehow*—Maddie was moving, gliding effortlessly over to where Kristopher was standing, her voice a warm bright ring. 'Are we good?'

'One minute to go.' Kris's eyes flicked to his, then fixed on Maddie again. 'Are you still eating outside?'

'Yes.' She turned, trapping him in a mischievous gaze. 'You okay with that?'

He nodded, willing his blood to pump in reverse, willing Kristopher's gaze not to drift any lower than his face. 'Of course.'

'Good.' She came towards him, skirt swirling, then breezed on past. 'Come on, then, let's go sit.'

She was killing him.

He followed her outside. No dining table. No chairs. Just the hurricane lamps throwing their warm glow over the decking and the Lshaped rattan sofa unit with its low square table on which there were two napkins, two glasses and a bottle of red, uncorked.

Not what he'd been expecting. He met her eye. 'What is this?'

'Informal dining.' She twinkled a smile, then picked up the wine bottle and put it into his hands. 'I thought it'd be just the thing after a long day spent doing unmentionable things to an elephant. Will you pour?'

He felt a slow spreading warmth, a smile unwinding inside. So nice being with her. So easy, so familiar. But also, confusing as hell. And there wasn't even space right now to sort out his thoughts because she was looking at him, expecting him to do something useful with the wine.

'Sure.' He glanced at the bottle. 'Are you okay with this?'

'Absolutely.' She was settling herself onto a sofa, drawing her legs up. 'I have a wider range these days, but in any case, this is about you and what you like.' Her voice dipped low, softening. 'I know you chose the Sauvignon Blanc for me the other night.'

His heart pulsed. What to say? He had. She knew it. So many things they knew about each other and so many they didn't. Like why she hadn't come back. But letting that thought coil tight was going to spoil things. She was making an effort here, for him. He needed to pin himself to the present and enjoy it.

He poured and set the bottle down. 'You're right, I did choose it for you—'

And then a flash of white caught the edge of his vision. He turned, and suddenly all the tightness inside was loosening. Was this real? Was Kristopher actually coming out with an enormous, sizzling pizza?

He felt his belly starting to vibrate, a chuckle filling his throat. Had Maddie asked his Michelin-starred chef to make pizza? Only she could have done that. Only her. He looked over. She was giggling, her eyes dancing, full of irresistible light.

'What are you thinking, Kade? Good idea or epic fail?'

Maddie! Too funny. Too perfect.

He felt a fresh smile bursting onto his cheeks. 'Good idea. Definitely!'

'Well, that properly hit the spot.' Kaden was topping up their glasses, still smiling like a kid at Christmas.

'I thought it might…' His chef, his ingredients, but still organising it had felt good, had felt like she was giving him something back for all his kindness, for the way he was protecting her from the other journalists even though he didn't think they were a threat, for the way he'd held her when she'd been upset, both times. But it wasn't only to thank him for all the things he was doing for her. It was also for that stricken look he'd had on his face when Jerry had radioed in the news. In that moment she'd felt the weight of the responsibility he was carrying, the immensity of Masoka and everything that went with it. As soon as she'd got back, doing something nice for him was all she'd been able to think about, to bolster him, to show him that she was in his camp. And if it hadn't been for the journalist who apparently wasn't being stoic, then maybe it would have been working too. As it was, she could see a journalist-shaped shadow hovering at his back, and she wasn't convinced that the champagne he'd sent was going to chase it away. Or maybe that was just her. Maybe other travel writers did accept 'gifts,' in which case, maybe everything would be all right.

'Why?' He was lifting up her glass, holding it out. 'Have I been walking around with pizza-hungry eyes?'

She felt the brief scorch of his fingertips as she took it. 'Not exactly, but you always used to crave pizza after rugby, and it struck me that wrestling an elephant was likely to be a bit of a scrum, so, you know, it figured.'

'Intuitive!' He put his glass to his lips, smiling. 'Funnily enough, I can't remember the last time I had pizza.'

'Me neither.' She smiled to mask a little sinking feeling. 'Most of the time it's fine dining.'

His eyebrows flashed. 'Knives and forks.'

'Yes, lovely food but...' She didn't want to dampen the mood but there was something about sitting here with him in the mellow glow of the lamps that was making her want to talk, and maybe he wasn't interested, maybe that's why he'd hardly asked her anything about herself, but right now she didn't care. She wanted to talk to him like she'd used to, letting her cracks show, because he was safety, the one she'd always been able to talk to. She put her glass down. 'But I miss this, you know. Lounging in comfy clothes, eating pizza...' She felt her ribs tightening. Did she dare to push the thought over the line, say it out loud? His eyes were narrowing into hers, interested, gently prompting. She took a breath. 'I miss having someone to eat pizza with.'

'Someone?' For a long moment his eyes held her and then slowly his face stiffened. 'What on earth am I supposed to do with that?'

Her heart stumbled. Pain in his eyes, *finally*,

bright, and obvious. Is this what she wanted, is this what she was about, goading him, prodding the sore spot to see how deep it went? She felt a filtering darkness, something stirring. Yes. *Yes!* Having a showdown hadn't been part of the plan but somehow half a bottle of Pinot Noir had brought her here and there was no going back now. She didn't want to. She wanted to face this, had to know. She had to measure what she'd done to him because otherwise how could she ever make amends, put them back together again? She swallowed hard. Because that's what she was thinking about, wasn't it? Fixing them. Subconsciously, it's why she'd put on her flirty jumpsuit that first night, why she'd provoked him into tickling her when they'd been watching the dogs. Everything she'd done was about getting behind his gaze to see what the chances were of putting things right.

She ran her eyes over his face. But that thought had only suggested itself because of what he was projecting. It wasn't just her. He was driving things too, responding to her cues. That game of tag he'd started before dinner, heat in his eyes, that loaded moment. God knows, if he'd been cool and distant from the outset, if he hadn't pulled her into his arms in that lovely warm way at the airstrip, she'd have been sitting in her Lina James box right now instead of sitting with him here under a starlit sky. So it wasn't all her. He was here. She was here. And maybe right now he was angry but that was okay. He had the right to be.

'I mean, seriously...' His tongue travelled across his lower lip. 'What do you want me to say?' He lifted his chin, mouth twisting. 'Am I supposed to feel sorry for you?'

Her heart clenched. His eyes were wet at the edges. *Her fault.* She'd caused him this pain, and she was going to take it all, everything he needed to lay at her door. She'd see him through to the other side because on the other side there was love. She could feel it and that's the only thing that mattered.

She took a breath, tightening her gaze on his. 'No—'

'Because I was there for you, Mads, always. I *was* your someone, but you...' He was shaking his head now, twisting his glass back and forth. 'You didn't come back. You didn't give me a chance.' His eyes emptied. 'Why? Why didn't you come back? All those plans we made...' His voice was cracking, tearing her heart out. 'Uni... Edinburgh...not to mention the small matter of for ever. Remember that?' His gaze sharpened. 'Remember?'

Hiding under forbidden daytime covers, that so soft light and the warm smell of his skin, their bodies mingling, tangling, the taste of his mouth, seeing nothing beyond the glow in his eyes, words rising, floating free in whispers.

'This is for ever, Kade, you and me. For ever...'

Suddenly his glass was clattering down, and he was getting up, his voice mounting. 'I would have walked through fire and back for you, do you know that? Do you?' He was grinding out words, leaving her no space to interject. 'Wasn't it clear enough? Didn't I say it often enough? I mean, *how* couldn't you have known?' His eyes were loud, practically pulsing into hers, and then suddenly they were filling again. 'You didn't have to be alone. You could have had me...' And then his gaze was retreating, his voice shading back to bitterness. 'But I guess I wasn't enough...'

She felt a black hole opening up inside, her organs disappearing into it. How could he think that?

Because you let him.

'Let's just get it over with, shall we.' He moved to the veranda rail, wanting to distance himself no doubt. 'You found someone else in Paris, didn't you?' His hands flapped. 'And you figured that, what?' Bruised eyes blazed into hers. 'Kaden's a clever guy. He'll work it out for himself eventually?'

'No!' Her heart cracked. 'I didn't… I never…'

Breathe! You are here, you are alive, you are going to fix this.

She got up and went to stand in front of him, loading her gaze with everything, loading her voice. 'You're so wrong.' His eyebrows flickered faintly. 'I can see why you think it but you're wrong. There was no one in Paris.' She could feel her sinuses growing hot. 'There's never been anyone.'

'Never?' His throat was working. 'No one?'

'No.'

'I don't understand.' His fingers went to his eyebrow. 'So if there wasn't…then why? Why the hell…' He seemed to run out of words. The rest was in his eyes, shock, confusion, incredulity and…a flicker of something that looked like warmth coming back.

She felt that warmth turning her inside out. Why indeed? Because looking at him now, all the reasons she'd clung to so tightly didn't make sense. But then maybe making sense didn't matter any more. What was important was talking. Explaining.

She took a breath. 'Believe me, ever since I got here, I've been asking myself the same question.' His lips parted slightly, and she felt a tug, a stab of desperate longing. 'I see you now, the same as you always were, but… I got it into my head that you wouldn't want…'

'What…?' Suddenly his hands were on her shoulders, warm and gentle, his eyes reaching in. 'What wouldn't I have wanted?'

She felt a burn starting. 'I thought you wouldn't want to have anything to do with me, because of Dad, because of your family being so upright.' He was frowning, shaking his head, but she had to finish. 'I was so ashamed, Kade. I still am. Overnight Dad was a stranger—a criminal—and Mum was telling me not to trust anyone, not to contact anyone. All of a sudden, I was in Paris living with a woman I'd only ever met twice before, and I couldn't talk to you…' The burn was scalding her eyes now, prickling. 'I couldn't see you. My heart was breaking, and I couldn't *do* anything, *change* anything. And then, after Dad was sent down, I don't know, everything felt so hard, the thought of slotting back in. I wanted to see you, but I just couldn't face you, in case you'd changed, in case you didn't want me.'

'No, Maddie, no.' His voice was cracking. 'How could you have ever thought—'

'I was so knocked back, that's how! I couldn't see any good in the world. Just getting out of bed in the morning was an effort. I wasn't sleeping. I still don't. It would have killed me if you'd given me the cold shoulder, Kade. It seemed easier to go forward, to become a different person, than to go back—' his eyes were swimming, making hers swim too, making a sob swell in her throat '—but I never stopped loving you, you've got to believe me, so don't ever think that, okay, just don't!'

'Oh, God, Madeleine, Maddie...' He was looking at her as if he couldn't take enough of her in and then suddenly his hands were cupping her face and he was lowering his mouth to hers.

She felt her breath stopping and then her heart. Same tingle, same warm perfect lips, same clean skin smell, but there was that soft rub of stubble now, that extra height, that irresistible manliness. Her heart struck up again. Was this happening too fast? Should she be resisting? Maybe, but she couldn't think of a reason to, not while his lips were moving over hers, teasing hers apart, making heat rise and liquid pool. She didn't want to resist. What she wanted was exactly this—him—right here, right now, with every fibre of her being.

She caught his face, kissing him back, parting her lips for his tongue, feeling its wet heat working its magic with every firm stroke, bringing her core to tingling life, her nipples, her skin, the roots of her hair. She could feel her body trembling, her pulse rushing, then slowing, then pulsing thick and hot. He smelt so good, felt so good. She couldn't get enough. She slid her hands down his neck, over his shoulders, felt him responding, pulling her closer, pressing himself hard against her so she could feel every hot throbbing inch of him.

'I. Have. Missed. You. With. All. Of. My. Heart.' He was filling her mouth with the words as his hands roamed, caressing her breasts, circling her nipples, then sliding down, one hand under her buttocks, the other between her legs.

She went for her waistband, but his hands were already there, tugging it down. The linen whispered against her legs as it fell, and then his hand was back, his palm hot, moving slowly. She closed her eyes, clinging to his shoulders as he slid his hand inside her G-string, whimpering as his fingers began to move. He groaned a low groan, stubble grazing her ear. 'You feel so sweet.' His fingers zoned in, lingering, circling. 'So incredibly wet.' She felt her pulse spike, an explosion of heat in her veins. Teasing fingers. Well-timed words. He was killing her softly. Like he always did. She could feel her control going, her senses skewing. It was too sweet. Too bitter. Bittersweet. But somehow words were forming, coming out.

'Don't stop, Kade, please don't stop...'

But he was doing what he always used to do, delivering just enough to keep her hanging on a pulse beat, dangling, and then he released her, finally, and she was tipping over the edge, seeing stars, shaking around his fingers, trembling, then falling back, coming down.

'Oh, God, Maddie.' He was kissing her again, softly now, deeply, making her head spin all over again.

'Kaden…' She put her hands to his face, wanting to say something, but somehow words weren't enough.

His lips came to hers again. 'It's okay, I know.' And then he was leaning away, hazy-eyed, smiling. 'Let's take this inside.'

CHAPTER EIGHT

KADEN BLINKED AWAKE. Sharp fingers of sunlight were poking through the shutters, prodding at the walls. So different to the pale glow of dawn. He turned his head, felt warmth blooming in his chest. Maddie was asleep, hair mussed, a slight flush in her cheeks. No wonder. They'd seen in daybreak with a last, slow assault on each other's bodies before finally curling up, exhausted.

He shifted onto his side so he could look at her. Sweet lips, that feathery sweep of her lashes. Seeing her like this, lost to the world, her expression peaceful, it was hard to believe she was an insomniac. His belly pulsed. Peter Saint James had a lot to answer for, the treasury man with the opposite of the Midas touch, laying waste to hearts, minds, lives. Maddie had been so full of light and life, and now... He slid his hand across the pillow touching her hair with one finger. She was still full of light and life, but she was also damaged. Wary, fearful, so knocked back that she'd thought he wouldn't want to see her, that he'd have turned his face away if she'd reappeared. Wrong, as far as he was concerned, but still, there was some truth in what she'd said, wasn't there? He only had to think of his own father and that miserable Eurostar journey back to London...

'Look, son. I know you think you're in love, but you mustn't look for her—do you hear me? You mustn't. We need to keep away from that family. There's a lot at stake. God, Kaden, we've had Peter and Natalie over for dinner because of you kids, but now they want to question me too. "Routine," they're calling it. They're going to be asking me if Peter ever alluded to any of his property dealings, if he ever mentioned any names...'

Which, thank goodness, he hadn't, but Dad's face had been grey all the same, and he hadn't deserved to be burdened like that, not when he and Mum had only been trying to be friendly with Maddie's parents because of *him*, because Maddie was his girlfriend and had been for two years by that time.

But if his own father, a good man—decent— had been telling him to forsake Maddie, then there'd have been others, withdrawing, making polite excuses. Facing that, enduring that, after everything she'd already been through, when her anxiety levels were ramped so high that she was having panic attacks, must have felt impossible for her. He got it. At least, in his head he did.

He rolled over, staring up into the white gauze of the mosquito nets. Last night he hadn't been thinking. Emotion had swept in and taken him over. There she'd been, crying, telling him that she'd never stopped loving him, that there'd never been anyone else, and he'd cracked like a shell, lapped it all up. It had been impossible not to kiss her, impossible not to want to love her. And it had felt so right. All night long it had felt right between them. No holding back, bodies and words flowing. *I love you. I love you*, they'd said to each other over and over. His heart twisted. But she'd said it before, hadn't she, then stayed away, and even though he understood her reasons all the way to his bones, one hundred percent, there was a small voice in his head whispering that if she'd loved him enough she'd have come back to him, whatever it took, that just because she was saying it now didn't mean she wouldn't leave him again.

Cruel voice.

He couldn't listen. Didn't want to.

He eased himself out of the bed, pulled on

his jeans and slipped through the doors onto the veranda.

The sun was well up. Warm. Tempered by a faint breeze. He glanced at his bare wrist. His watch was inside somewhere, along with his shirt, and his shoes, and his heart. *Oh, God!* What to think? How to feel? Last night had been sublime, feeling her again, so close, her fingers trailing, the sweet taste of her mouth. When he'd been walking here yesterday, he'd never imagined that he'd still be here this morning, never in a million years have imagined that he and Maddie would spend the night making love, feeling so present, so alive, crying out with it, not caring, because they'd always been vocal, always let it all out. But now what?

He went to the rail, lifting his gaze to the tree-tops. What did he want? In spite of his doubts, in spite of everything, did he still want her? His heart stopped, then started again. Yes, with every beat of his heart, but there was so much to consider. In many ways they were the same as they'd always been, but they were both different too. Twelve years older, twelve years different. She had her Lina James life, lonely perhaps, but still it was the life she'd made. She had a diary full of commitments and obligations. And he was here in the back of beyond building the dream he'd invented to replace her, but this dream was his life now, and not just his. He had his staff's lives to think about too, obligations of his own, projects on the go. Every cent was invested, every ounce of his energy.

Would Maddie ever want this? Would Masoka suit her, the wildlife, the insects? Would this life appeal to the girl who'd stumbled backwards because of a tadpole? And if it wasn't the place for her, could he see himself giving it all up for her? An ache bounced between his temples. So many questions. How could he even begin to answer them when the world was skewed on its axis, when his heart and his mind and his body were reeling?

'Hello, you.' The warm shock of her arms going round him gave way to a different kind of heat as her breasts melted against his back. He felt the soft press of her lips on his shoulder blade. 'You left me.'

He swivelled to face her, feeling his breath catch. Still mussed, still naked, even more beautiful than he remembered. He pulled her in. 'I left you to sleep.'

'I was sleeping, wasn't I?' She smiled up at him. 'I can't remember the last time I slept till after ten.'

Not his usual thing either but since Maddie had arrived, nothing had felt remotely usual. He kissed her nose. 'Not wanting to rain on your parade or anything, but we didn't go to sleep until six. We've had four and half hours, tops!'

She tossed her head coquettishly as if she still had her Tresses mane. 'And yet I feel so good.' Mischief darted through her gaze. 'There's clearly some strange alchemy at work.'

Love in her eyes. Unmistakable. Real.

He felt his heart lifting, a smile breaking loose. 'You can call it that if you like.'

'By any other name, huh?' Her eyebrows flickered, and then she was sliding her hands up and around his neck. 'So anyway, what does a girl have to do around here to get some breakfast?'

Those eyes. Those lips.

'Well…' He bent his head, tasting her mouth for a long, tingling moment. 'The dining room is closed now so a girl would have to order room service—'

Except that would mean Precious delivering a tray along with more of those deep knowing looks, the ones she'd been giving him ever since he'd asked her to deliver Maddie's note. And then, of course, Kristopher would be the one preparing the breakfast, Kristopher who'd seemed to be smiling in stereo last night. And what about Chanda? And Jerry? They'd hear about it, not that it would be breaking news because they both knew that he never took anyone on a one-to-one game drive.

Basically, his whole staff must know by now that there was something special about Lina James. They'd pop if they knew the truth, but he couldn't tell them anything yet because nothing was resolved. It's not as if he and Maddie had spent the night talking. He held in a sigh. But they needed to, needed to talk, and to listen to each other. It seemed heavy in a way, getting into all that after just one night, but then they *were* heavy, weren't they, heavy with history, and for him, there was that tiny speck of insecurity that he'd like not to be feeling. Talking was the answer, but maybe not here, under the watch of kind but curious eyes. Somewhere else. Somewhere where it would be just the two of them with a skeleton staff who were used to keeping themselves invisible. He felt a smile coming. Lucky for him he had such a place.

He kissed her again.

'—or we could go out for breakfast.'

'Out?' Her eyebrows flickered. 'Out where?'

He felt his lips twitching. 'Somewhere.'

'Intriguing.' She was scrunching her face at him, miming inscrutable. 'And what should I wear for this somewhere breakfast?'

He couldn't hold in a chuckle. 'More than

you're wearing at the moment would be fine, at least for the journey.'

She was laughing now, eyes sparkling. 'I don't know what you're planning but I'm getting a good feeling.'

Good feelings. Warm feelings. They were the feelings he was getting too, the feelings he wanted to run with, to believe in, but talking was the only way he was going to get there, and they needed to be at Tlou for that. The sooner the better.

'Hold on to that thought.' He freed himself from her arms, backstepping towards the doors. He'd call ahead, ask the staff to prepare fruit salad and pancakes. She'd always loved pancakes, with maple syrup, and a drizzle of cream. And he'd ask them to find a jug too, a nice big one!

Her lips quirked. 'You're looking mighty pleased with yourself all of a sudden.'

He grinned. 'It's probably got something to do with the view…'

'Oh…' She pivoted a little, arching her back, eyeing him over her shoulder. 'You mean this view?'

Long legs. Smooth, shapely buttocks. He felt heat stirring in his groin, a powerful urge to sweep her up and take her back to bed. But going back to bed wouldn't get them to Tlou, would it? And that's where they needed be. At Tlou, there'd be plenty of time for everything, loving, talking. God, after all these years it felt like a dream come true, the prospect of being alone with her, just the two of them.

He forced his eyes upwards to meet her teasing gaze. 'Exactly that view, as well you know.' She was going to be so thrilled with Tlou, the whole *Out of Africa* thing, but he wasn't going to tell. Keeping her dangling was so much more fun. 'You get ready. I'll see you out front in twenty.' He stepped back, faking an afterthought. 'Oh, and you'll need an overnight bag.'

She looked over, felt her heart skipping for the hundredth time. Kaden was perfection. Thick copper hair blowing back from his forehead, shades perched on that fine straight nose, lips just the right amount of full, lips that had always fitted to hers so perfectly. What was he up to? Did she even care? She felt a sudden luxurious warmth unfurling inside. No, because whatever he was planning was making him smile and his smile was more than enough. Contagious. She could feel it aching in her own cheeks. Her body was aching too, in the sweetest way, because of him. She bit down on her lip, feeling a bubble of happiness fizzing through her veins. Had she really just spent an entire night making love with this gorgeous man, this man who also happened to be the love of her life? Yes, with bells on! Those tanned hands, loose on the wheel; maybe they did venture into some unsavoury places, but it's the last thing she'd been thinking about last night when they'd been moving over her body, lingering, caressing. Those hands. Those fingers. They still seemed to know everything about her, how to bring her to the brink, how to tip her over the edge. Muscle memory.

She felt a quiver low down in her belly and looked away, stretching her gaze to the *veld*. Thinking about clever hands was only stirring her up, and getting herself all stirred up while they were bouncing along to Kaden's mysterious breakfast venue was pointless. Better to be concentrating on the waving yellow grass, and the scrub, and the wildlife, all things she needed to write about in her blog piece, which was still there to do, even though things had taken a turn.

She lifted her eyes to the sky. So wide. So blue. Had it looked quite this wide, quite this blue, before? Had the herd of giraffe she'd seen from Jerry's Land Cruiser looked quite as graceful as the animals that were busy lolloping through the acacia beside them? No, and no, and no. Today everything was looking better, sounding better, feeling better, because of Kaden. *Oh, God!* How could she focus on the landscape when there was this feeling inside? Love, topped up so it was brimming, spilling out. Impossible to hide, impossible to hold in. Last night, she'd laid it all out so he would know that she loved him, had never stopped loving him. And all through the night she'd told him over and over again. And he'd said it back, eyes blazing with it. *'I love you, Maddie.'*

She looked over again, feeling warmth surging. Were they really falling back into place? It's what it felt like, but there was still so much to say and to work through. Saying *I love you* to Kaden was easy because it was true, but it didn't mean that everything else would be easy. Where did they go from here? This place was his life, his passion. Asking him to share it with her, asking him to let her in on the strength of one blissful night, felt audacious, even if it's what she wanted. Yes, he seemed to have understood why she'd let him go, but the hurt he'd poured out to her last night had deep roots. It had been there in his eyes, and there'd still be fragments left, words jumbling in a corner in his mind saying that in spite of everything she *should* have contacted him, that her love for him should have trumped everything. Nothing she hadn't thought herself, tortured herself with, over the years. But thinking about it now was too hard. Hard thoughts were nothing next to the allure of just diving in and drowning, splashing around in all the love, and the joy, and the happiness, feeling the bright zing of it, zinging the bright feel of it. No sleepwalking here, not a chance! She felt a smile rising inside. Probably not much sleep ahead either but what did sleep matter when her senses were trilling.

You are here. You are alive. You are safe. You're in love.

'You okay?' His eyes caught hers over the top of his shades.

She felt a tingle prickling to life, travelling up her spine. Something in his gaze was conjuring a memory...those limousines...those long rides home...the game they'd used to play... Her pulse skipped. Did she dare? She felt her pulse skipping again, then drumming, beating fast. It's not as if there was anyone to see them, and maybe he wouldn't bite anyway. Her belly clenched. But if he did...if he did, then it was no less than she deserved. She was twelve hungry years behind the curve. That was a lot of catching up.

She pressed her lips together, holding in a smile. 'I think so.'

A familiar light ignited behind his gaze. 'You *think* so?' His hand fell from the wheel, landing on her thigh. 'What does that mean?'

She felt her insides vibrating and tightening

at the same time. Laughter wanting to come and something else too. She pushed up her sunglasses, fastening her eyes on his. 'It means I'm not sure...'

His chin dipped. 'Could I do something to help?' His hand slid upwards, exerting a tantalising pressure. 'I mean, you're a cherished Masoka guest. I want you to be one hundred percent okay and to be absolutely sure about it.'

She bit her lips together hard. She could feel her body responding to his words, to his touch. She shifted a little, detecting wetness between her legs. 'What do you suggest?'

His eyebrows flickered and then suddenly the vehicle was slewing to a stop, bowling dust into the air. He removed his sunglasses, setting them on the dash carefully, and then he sat back, gesturing to his lap. 'I suggest you come to sit here.' His eyes darkened a little. 'Just slide on over.'

She felt a giggle coming. How could she ever have imagined that he wouldn't bite when he always had? She shot a glance at the handbrake. 'It's going to be more of clamber.'

'Here, let me...' In one swift movement strong hands were reaching under her, scooping her up, and before she could blink, she was sitting astride him, feeling the intimate warmth of his thighs beating through the fabric of her skirt. His eyes lit with a smile. 'Hello there.'

And then his hands were moving, travelling up her arms to the straps of her vest. He hooked his fingers in, eyes dancing. 'Do we like these?' She felt her breath hitching low down in her throat, and in the far distance, a smile tingling. *Game on!* She shook her head, holding his gaze. His eyes flashed. 'Didn't think so.' He lifted the straps off her shoulders, pulling the garment down, freeing her arms one by one, until she was naked to the waist. She felt her mouth drying, her pulse thundering. 'Comfy?' His gaze was playful, darkening, and then his hands connected with her breasts, his thumbs tracking a slow route over her nipples, once, twice, three times. She felt her breath catching, her back arching involuntarily, white-hot darts arrowing into her core. *Clever thumbs.* She wanted to stay, clinging to the moment, losing herself in it, but that's not how it worked. It was her turn now, to tease him back.

With difficulty she blinked him into focus and locked on, catching her lower lip between her teeth. 'Actually, no…' She moved, keeping the movement small, watching its effect on his face. 'I'm not quite comfy yet…' His lips parted in a low gasp. She shifted again, moving her hips, closing in by degrees until she could feel his full hard length right up against her. 'Oh, dear…' She rocked against him, feeling her pulse responding, thickening, seeing his focus hazing. She exhaled against his forehead, holding in a smile. 'There seems to be something in the way.' She pushed against him again, eliciting a low groan of pleasure that made her insides clench.

'Really…?' His voice sounded tight.

'Yes.' She brushed her lips over his, going for his button, undoing it. 'It might need some further investigation.' She sucked his lower lip into her mouth, feeling him opening, surrendering, feeling her limbs turning to liquid. 'Just this now…' She toyed with the tag of his zip, waiting for a beat before giving it a tug, because rushing had never been part of the game. He let out a heavy sigh as she freed him, a sigh that yanked tight a string of nerves in her core. She stroked him, feeling her focus narrowing. Hot, rigid, silky. He felt so good. She wanted to take him into her mouth, but the steering wheel was behind, trapping her. That left her hands, her fingertips, a little imagination. She stroked the pad of her finger across the liquid tip of him, felt her pulse spiking as an animal noise erupted from his throat. She swallowed hard, doing it again, and again, tormenting him, tormenting herself, until suddenly she couldn't stand it. 'Kade—'

'I hear you.' He started pushing at her skirt, trying to hold it away. 'Can you manage?'

She went for her underwear, felt her knee shearing off the seat. 'I can't...'

'Hang on.' His arm was going round her, holding firm. 'Right, lean.'

She leaned, letting his strength take her, feeling laughter suddenly vibrating through him, which set her off laughing too. He was tugging at her G-string, wrangling it down between fits and bursts, until finally, it twanged over her foot. He gasped against her. 'God, this was so much simpler in the limo.'

She felt another giggle shaking loose. 'You're not quitting, are you?'

'After all this effort?' He was levering her upright again. 'No way! I offered you one hundred percent satisfaction, and I'm going to deliver it.' And then his face fell. Suddenly he was blinking, looking confounded. 'Damn it, Mads, I'm sorry, but I didn't exactly come prepared for extra vehicular activity.'

A good name for their old game.

She twisted, reaching into the footwell for her bag, feeling a little glow of satisfaction. 'Well, lucky for us, I'm a regular Girl Scout. I grabbed some goodies out of the bathroom at the lodge, just in case.'

His face was incredulous. 'In case we got jiggy in the car?'

'Not specifically, but—' she felt a giggle

shaking free as she tore the foil and eased the condom over him '—it's been known is all I'm saying.'

His gaze heated, then softened. 'Certainly has. For the record, you're a genius.' And then his mouth was on hers, warm and urgent. 'Time to finish what we started.' She could feel his hands going underneath her, lifting her, steadying her, and then it was easing herself down, feeling her short breaths running out, her awareness narrowing to the deep, delicious connection, the sensation of being two in one. She closed her eyes. Moving could wait. This deep feeling was too heavenly, too warm, too perfectly intimate, to break.

'Look at me, Maddie.' His voice was low, compelling. She opened her eyes into his, felt her breath catching on his molten copper gaze. His thumbs moved over her cheekbones. 'I love you.' And then he was pulling her in, taking her lips, teasing with his tongue, reigniting the flames until she couldn't not move, couldn't not rock. And it was too divine, this slow moving, this pulsing of skin, and heart, this building ache, beating onwards like a drum. And then he was moving too, with her, meeting her, making the ache inside ache more. And his kiss was deepening, his tongue scorching hers, stroking hers to the rhythm of their bodies. She felt a cry filling her lungs from the inside, his body driving into hers, deeper and deeper, pushing her higher and higher onto a sublime wave that wouldn't stop rising. 'C'mon, baby, come on.'

Her breath stopped, her senses spiralling upwards again. His voice always did that, pushing her higher, but it was too much, this hanging, trembling on the edge. She needed it to stop, needed release. 'Please, Kaden, please...'

His mouth softened against hers momentarily. 'I love you, Maddie.' And then he was pushing, and she could feel herself going, tipping over the edge, everything tingling and clenching, and she could feel him releasing too, his body pulsing into hers, both of them gasping, trembling, holding on tight, shimmering back down to earth. For a long moment there was stillness and closeness and the warmth of his cheek against hers, and then sounds were filtering in, and smells. Dust, sweet grass.

'Wow.' His cheek twitched against her suddenly. 'I was not expecting this.'

She nuzzled in, feeling a smile coming. 'In spite of strong evidence to the contrary, neither was I—'

'I don't mean that.' He produced a low chuckle. 'I mean the audience.'

What?

She yanked up her vest and twisted round,

heart going, and then she felt her insides buckling, laughter bubbling. Beyond the hood, a herd
of impala was standing, their eyes locked on,
ears twitching. She bit down hard on her lips.
'Do you think they saw?'

'Yep.' Kaden was shaking with laughter now,
tears running down his face. 'Some of them
have got actual popcorn.'

CHAPTER NINE

'I CAN'T BELIEVE that Tlou didn't even cross my mind, not even when you said to bring an overnight bag.' Maddie was trailing her fingers over his chest, tracing little circles. She lifted her head, kissing him softly. 'You've clearly addled my brain.'

He felt a smile unwinding. 'More than your brain, I hope.'

'Oh, yes.' It was a heavily laden, yes, accompanied by a deep, mischievous look. 'Believe me, you've left no stone unturned.' Her lips grazed his again, setting off a jumping jack in his veins. 'I'm addled from head to toe.' She nuzzled her face into his neck. 'You're very good at addling, always were.'

'Right back at you.' Which was why they hadn't set foot out of the tent since breakfast, why the super-king-size with the canopy drawn around—*'more romantic,'* according to Maddie—had been their sole domain for the past four hours.

He ran his fingers along her arm, felt her snuggling in. The problem was that making love with Maddie was the only thing he wanted to do. She made him feel alive, present, not neutral, like Fran. He drew an uncomfortable breath. Poor Fran. What they'd had was nothing to this and he should have known, should never have let it continue. And Fran should have known too. Or maybe Maddie was right. Maybe Fran hadn't noticed because her heart had never properly been his either. Perhaps her heart had always belonged to the dream of Africa. It's what they'd started with after all, what they'd always had in common. Maybe, at least partly, that's where her tears had come from that day. Not crying for him so much as for everything that went with him, the work they were doing together, the passion they shared for the *bushveld* life.

He held in a sigh. Crossed wires, tangled emotions. Too late now to be pondering all that. Now Maddie was back and, no question, his heart was all the way in. He was beyond addled. God, she'd even had him in the Land Cruiser with the impala watching!

He closed his eyes. Limos. Land Cruisers. Whatever. When it came to Maddie, he was a lost cause. Every time she touched him with that look in her eyes, he could feel the tunnel opening up, sucking him in all over again. Maybe this was the phase they had to go through to get to the next one, the one that involved talking and planning a new for ever. It's what he wanted: a new for ever with her, and he wanted to tell her, read her reaction, hear her say it back. It's what he'd brought her here to do, what he'd imagined them doing alongside the loving, but bringing it up was hard. It felt like a too-high step.

He felt a band tightening around his chest. But it did, still, need to be resolved because way off in the distance, several times removed, he could feel his nerves chiming, a cold fear rinsing through his heart. Old hurt breeding new insecurity. How deep was her love? How true? Deep and true enough to see them through this time? That's what he really wanted to ask her, but how could he? It would only put his doubt on show, make her think that he didn't believe the reasons she'd given him for staying away. Good reasons. He could see it. She'd been so young, so uprooted, and the world was cruel. It all made sense, and yet that insecure speck inside kept jumping up, trying to bite him.

Ridiculous though, surely, because there was no reason on earth for her to vanish again. She knew now that he didn't care about Peter's mistakes or about his release from prison or about his shameless cash-in-on-a-scandal book. He'd told her straight that none of it reflected on her. She just had to believe it—believe him—shake off the shame she'd taken onto her own shoulders. She had to believe that she wasn't tainted, wasn't worth less, because of her father.

His heart contracted. She wasn't worth less, but she *was* damaged, fragile in places. It's why he needed to pick a careful path through his doubts, why he needed to find the right way into the *What do we do now?* conversation. He could help her, show her that she was better than her father. He could give her a home, show her the meaning of love and loyalty. All she had to do was let him, but to get to that place, they needed to be digging into the scary stuff, communicating beyond the curtained boundaries of the super-king-size.

He turned to look at her, felt his heart filling. She was sleeping, and…she was here for three more days. Three. More. Days. That was plenty of time. The right moment for talking was bound to arise. He just needed faith, needed to slow himself right down and enjoy the ride, speaking of which—he squinted at his watch—they'd need to be on their way in less than an hour.

He felt a tingle, then a smile was coming. Another surprise, hopefully on point. He couldn't wait to see her face.

* * *

Was this actually happening? She felt a smile breaking free, a tingling thrill of happiness. Was she really rising into the air in a basket beneath a towering balloon, a balloon that Kaden was piloting? The burner above her head was roaring, throwing down warmth, and the guys standing by the truck below were laughing and waving, laughing at her openly, because she'd been as excited as a kid from the moment Kaden had pulled up at the launch site. The basket had been on its side at that point, the balloon half filled, the burner going full tilt. Now they were upright and rising fast. The truck and the laughing faces were getting farther away, and the view was expanding. Trees, scrub, red earth, yellow grass and, in the distance, the sun, glowing orange, low in the sky. Heartbreakingly beautiful. And Kaden had planned it, kept it a secret, even kept it secret that he was the pilot—him. It had only clicked after they'd clambered into the basket and the other three guys had stayed where they were. That's when the penny had dropped, along with her jaw.

She turned to look at him. Mischief glinting in his eyes, his smile still twitching with his magnificent surprise. 'Am I forgiven now?'

She felt a tug of guilt. She hadn't exactly

jumped for joy when he'd pulled her out of bed. For once she'd been hard asleep, reluctant to move, well, frankly, a bit moany, but he'd paid no attention. He'd plied her with strong coffee and a bag of freshly made *koeksisters* and bundled her into the Land Cruiser, telling her it would be worth it.

She wound her arms around him. 'You're forgiven to the max. The real question is, am I? I was a proper grump.'

He laughed roundly. 'You were, but I was prepared for some hefty grumbling. It's not like we've had a lot of sleep and you never did like being woken up...' One eyebrow ticked up. 'Remember that time after the Kingston Ball...?'

'Oh, God.' She let go of him as the memory surfaced, taking shape. 'When we fell asleep in the pavilion—'

'Starkers under a picnic blanket because we'd been having a little fun.'

She felt a smile coming. 'I remember.' They hadn't bargained on falling asleep afterwards, hadn't bargained on that sudden rattling at the door.

He was shaking his head, chuckling. 'You wouldn't move. You kept telling me to let you sleep and I was panicking big-time, trying to get you to get dressed, thinking it was old man Kingston about to walk in on us.'

Moonlight spilling through tall windows, Kaden's warm limbs suddenly untangling from hers, his low, urgent whispers tickling the edge of her consciousness. *'Maddie! Wake up, Maddie!'*

'I was tired. I'd had that early shoot, remember, and the punch was aptly named. Knocked me right out.'

'You never could take much alcohol...' A warm, indulgent look came into his eyes. 'Anyway, I managed to get you moving, *eventually.*'

'All for nothing too, if I remember rightly, because by the time we crept out, whoever it was had gone, so we could have stayed put.'

'But not this time.' He reached up, adjusting one of the burner levers. 'I'm guessing you wouldn't have wanted to miss this...'

'Definitely not.' She looked past his eyes and into vast innards of the balloon. Just nylon and hot air holding them aloft, but she felt safe. Always safe with him. She met his gaze again. 'I wouldn't have missed this for the world. It's incredible.'

A smile spread over his face and then his attention shifted. 'Check out the zebras.'

She followed his gaze and felt her breath catch. The animals were galloping, a herd of thirty or so, sleek-flanked, graceful, powdering the dust as they went. 'Are they running away from us, from the balloon, I mean?' Orange and white, with the black Masoka logo blazoned across. From a zebra's point of view probably alarming.

'I don't know, maybe. I can't see any sign of a predator.' He blasted more heat into the balloon and then his eyes came to hers. 'But then zebra spook quite easily, like horses, so it could be anything. Maybe they're just enjoying a canter.'

He looked so confident, so in control.

She turned back to the view. He'd achieved so much in twelve years, becoming a vet, then coming here, taking on this vast wild kingdom, launching what was clearly going to be a profitable business so he could stretch himself further, fund other, worthy endeavours. He'd spared no expense at Masoka, renovating the lodge to the highest degree, building luxury accommodations, and, as for the bush camp... Canvas, yes, but that's where the similarity to camping ended. The bed was vast, made up with impeccable linens, and the outdoor shower was a work of art with its polished copper fittings and a drench head the size of a dinner plate. Meals were freshly prepared and served by a contingent of staff who remained invisible at all other times. There had to be at least three of them, probably eight at the bigger bush camp, and maybe thirty more at the lodge. Guides, chefs, bar staff, housekeepers, managers, cleaners, pool people, spa therapists and beauticians. Kaden was employing a lot of people, and then there were contractors too, the builders who were building the schools and medical centres he was putting into the local communities.

And with all those plates spinning, he'd still, somehow, learned to pilot a hot-air balloon. He was a force of nature, always had been. Full of ideas, full of energy and passion. He'd filled these past twelve years to the brim and there was bound to be more, because Kaden had always been a 'more' kind of guy.

She bit her lips. There was so much to discover in him, so much she wanted to know, but it was going to take time and time wasn't her friend. She was supposed to be leaving in three days. Her stomach clenched. She didn't want to go, but how to say it, how to steer the conversation that way? And even if she managed it, asking to stay felt like a demand she didn't exactly have the right to make, not after having stayed away like she had, causing him all that pain. Not her fault, plenty of reasons, but facts were facts. She *had* hurt him, and now they were in the throes of whatever this was, talking about love, acting like lovers, but the thought of putting a seal on it, even though it's what she wanted, was churning her up inside. What if things went wrong? What if she hurt him all over again?

She felt her heart contracting. She loved him so much. He didn't deserve to be hurt again, and it wouldn't be her intention, ever, but she wasn't the person she'd been. Yes, Kaden was safety. With him she could feel Madeleine Saint James coming back to life, shining bright, but she could also feel the snipped wires and jagged pieces inside, latent panic leaping like a flame. Who was Kaden in love with? The girl she'd been, or the woman she was now? Any conversation about the future had to take account of the woman she was now, but how to do that when she didn't know herself who that woman was. It was all too hard to think about. If only she could stay in this moment, suspended in the dream she'd been living ever since he'd kissed her last night. If this moment could last for ever, then everything would be perfect.

'Mads…' His voice broke into her thoughts. 'What are you thinking?'

Her chest went tight. If only she dared to tell him her actual thoughts, get it over with, but she couldn't. Not yet.

She took a breath and turned to look at him. Eyes full of the sunset, full of warmth. It was a bolstering kind of warmth. She felt the tightness loosening a little, something steadying inside. 'I was just thinking that I still can't get over you with this balloon. I mean, there's got to be a story that goes with it, and then I was thinking that there must be so many stories...' She felt a burn starting behind her lids. 'Things I don't know, all the things I've missed.'

'Hey.' His hand closed over her shoulder. 'It's the same for me, with you.'

The tightness inside flexed, shrinking around a germ of bitterness. 'You haven't missed much where I'm concerned.' A life spent hiding—running—not connecting with anyone or anything. She swallowed hard. 'I'm a cul-de-sac.'

A frown flashed through his eyes. 'No, you're not! You're the strongest person I know. You took a devastating situation and you built back. You turned things around, carved out a career that loads of people would give their eyeteeth for. Queen of the elite travel scene is no small achievement.'

She felt something give. They were the things she told herself all the time to shore herself up but hearing them from Kaden's lips made them seem more real somehow, true even.

His gaze was softening with a smile. 'You're a powerful woman, Maddie. Think about it. You could make or break Masoka with a single well-aimed sentence!'

'I'm not going to break Masoka.'

'Pleased to hear it.' He squeezed her shoulder gently and then his hand went back to the lever above his head. 'Anyway, going for the silver lining, at least we've got plenty to talk about. We should embrace it, get digging and delving.'

Finding silver linings. That was Kaden. Force of nature!

'You're right.' She felt a lightening inside, her smile returning. 'So, honestly, I have to know, why ballooning, because in the whole time I knew you, ballooning never even broke the surface.'

'That's because it was never underneath. It was a total whim.' He blasted the burner briefly. 'When I was at Kruger there were some guys running an operation there. I used to go along sometimes to help them set up because it was something different. They took me up a few times and I loved it, so I found out about piloting, did the training and got myself a licence.'

'Just like that?'

'Yep.' He grinned. 'Then, when I took over here, it seemed like a no-brainer to put ballooning on the menu, not that I pilot the excursions. The guys who brought it out for us run the show on a day-to-day basis, but with a bigger basket. I just fly for fun in this little picnic basket.'

'I love your picnic basket. It's cosy.' And then suddenly she couldn't not slide her arms around him, couldn't not let her admiration flow free. 'You're quite something, Kaden Barr. Proud father to wild dog pups, intrepid vet, pilot of the skies and—' she couldn't resist '—red hot in the sack, as well as in at least two different types of vehicles.'

He laughed. 'What can I say?'

A spark of mischief flared. 'Have you ever—'

'No!' Instantly his hands were on her arms, putting her away from him. 'Don't even think about it. The balloon pilot's handbook is very clear about what is and isn't allowed in flight.'

'Okay.' She smothered a giggle and turned. 'I suppose I'll just have to content myself with this astonishing view.'

'Perfect! Hold that thought.'

She ran her eyes over the landscape. What a thought to hold, drifting through the sky with Kaden, birds gliding below, impala scattering with white tails flashing and, beyond, a small group of giraffes flowing sedately through a loose stand of thorn trees. She felt her heart swelling, a sigh escaping. 'It's just like *Out of Africa*. I can almost hear the score playing…'

And what else…? What else was playing in-

side her head? What was she seeing in the distance? A future, for them, here? A future with
him?

Stop!

This was crazy. He needed to put a lid on his
insecurity right now and focus on the moment.
They were having a good time. She was thrilled
with the balloon adventure, thrilled with the
views, and she'd just been propositioning him.
That was a thought worth holding on to.

He checked the burners, then went to stand
behind her, wrapping his arms around her shoulders. And this was another thought to hold on
to. Maddie melting against him all warm, safe
in his arms, right where he wanted her to be.

She twisted, looking up. 'Is this allowed?'

'Yes.' He kissed her, keeping it brief just
in case the tunnel sucked him in again. 'The
grouchy pilot says it's fine since we're nicely
on target for the landing site.'

She smiled, then turned back to the view. 'But
I don't want it to end.'

Neither did he, not while the sun was sliding towards the horizon like this, not while she
was here with him—impossibly—drifting over
his adopted home. A pang caught him in the
chest. Where was home for her? He didn't even
know. So many things they didn't know about
each other.

He buried his lips into her hair. 'Where do you live when you're not travelling?'

'Mum's place near Marseilles. She bought it after Dad was sentenced. It's got a little apartment on the top floor that I use as a bolthole.'

At least she had a base, and Natalie. He hugged her tighter. 'How is your mum?'

'Okay. Well, dismayed about Dad's book, not that she's said anything.' She wriggled, swivelling round to face him. 'We don't talk about him.' Her eyes clouded. 'He's a taboo subject.'

On whose insistence? He felt a frown coming. Sounded like Natalie was calling the shots and Maddie was, what, falling in, going along with it? Figured. Just yesterday she'd said that thing about how everything had been a million times worse for Natalie than for her. Had that mindfulness kept her from pushing her mum to talk about things? If so, it meant that Maddie had never got to talk about things either. No wonder she still had all that hurt, and hate, stuck inside.

'The book thing is so hard, not knowing what's in it...' She was chewing the edge of her lip which was the nervous thing she did when she wasn't twisting her pendant about. 'I mean, I really don't want to look at it in case there's personal stuff in there, but at the same time, if he's written about me and Mum, then there's a part of me that does want to know.'

Fear in her eyes, that scrawl of pain.

His heart seized. Why the hell couldn't Peter Saint James just disappear? Why couldn't he be the one hiding his face for shame? Didn't he care about Maddie, about the hurt he was causing? Didn't he have a scrap of imagination, a shred of decency inside? Unbelievable! He exhaled, pushing it down. Anger wasn't going help Maddie, wasn't going to take away her pain. Pain had to be managed, like with the elephant. Lance the abscess, drain the poison, then disinfect. Shift the dynamic towards healing. Maybe that was the answer, right there.

'Mads, I can't believe I'm saying this but maybe you should check it out. At least you'll know what you're dealing with.'

'Would you look?' Her gaze was wide, trusting. 'If it was your father, your father's book?'

'I think I'd have to, yes.' He felt his stomach tightening suddenly, his pulse gathering. Could this be the moment he'd been waiting for, the moment to talk about the future? It felt like it, felt like an opportunity. He took a gentle hold of her shoulders. 'You know, you don't have to be alone with this. We could order the book online, check it out together over a bottle of wine...' A light was coming on behind her gaze. Love. Gratitude. He licked his lips. Final push. 'The only thing is, there's no same-day delivery service out here so it would mean waiting.'

She blinked. 'Waiting…?'

'Yes, for a bit.' His mouth was drying. 'Or longer. It would be fine by me, if you wanted to wait…stay, I mean, for longer…for as long as…then I could be with you for the book and for—' He felt tightness cramping in his chest, panic rising. Why wasn't she saying anything? Did he need to be more emphatic? Maybe he just needed to be plain.

He licked the dryness off his lips. 'What I'm trying to say—ineptly—is that I don't want you to go, Mads, not when we've only just found each other again.' He put a hand to her face. 'I love you.'

For a moment she was still, and then her eyes were filling, tears sliding out. 'I don't want to go either, but the thing is, what's coming into my head right now is that I'm scared, scared of wrecking things, scared of hurting you again.' Her face was crumpling, tearing his heart out. 'I don't want to hurt you, not again.'

'Oh, Maddie.' He felt tenderness rushing in. 'You didn't hurt me on purpose.' And she hadn't stayed away because she didn't love him either. He could see it now, shimmering through her eyes, quivering on her lips. She was trapped inside her own fear and shame. If only Natalie had helped her more, let her talk, let her release it all, then maybe things would have been different and she'd have found a way back to him, but it was too late to worry about that now. The past was written. It was the future that mattered. He smoothed her tears away with his thumbs. 'We were dealt a bad hand, that's all, but we've got another chance.'

'We have, but I'm a mess, Kade. I know it.' She lifted his hands away from her face, and then her eyes were on his, shadows moving through. 'Parts of me are the same, but the sameness doesn't reach all the way in. There's all this other stuff going on inside, fear that feels like it's closing in, and I can't stop it, can't stop feeling it. I love you, Kade, I really do, and I want to think about what happens next, but there's a bigger part of me that wants to stay right here, *literally* in this moment, in this basket, drifting along, just the two of us. I don't think I can process more than this—'

'Which is why we need to take the pressure off.' He took hold of her hands. 'We need to give ourselves time to just be, time to fill in the blanks, find new feet and maybe to grow back.' Her gaze was filling again, softening, lifting his spirits, making his pulse fly. 'I'm talking about trying, that's all. No pressure. No promises. Just more time.' He felt a smile coming. 'More wild dog pups, more ballooning. You up for that?'

She was looking at him as if she couldn't fit enough of him in, and then she was smiling all the way to her eyes. 'What do you think?'

CHAPTER TEN

'WHAT ARE WE going to tell Chanda?'

'Nothing she hasn't already worked out for herself, I imagine.' Kaden's eyes came to hers, smiling eyes. 'I think we can assume that the whole staff is up to speed by now. Taking you to Tlou was a bit of a giveaway.'

And moving from her guest lodge into his rooms when they got back—in T minus ten minutes—was going to clinch it. But it wasn't quite what she'd meant. She stretched a hand to the back of his neck, playing with his hair, feeling a knot tightening inside. 'What I mean is, should we tell everyone my real name or what?'

'We'll tell them whatever you want, whatever you're comfortable with.'

The knot pulled tighter. Why hadn't she thought about this before, the actual practicalities of staying? Up there in the balloon, Kaden had made it all sound so easy, talking about adding time to take the pressure off. No promises.

No expectations. Just her, staying for longer, so they could keep catching up, keep filling in their blanks, so they could keep on loving each other. Trying to build back. At Tlou, believing in that dream, living it, had been easy too. Dining under the stars by the fire with a hundred lamps glowing, then bed…which hadn't involved a lot of sleeping but at least when sleep had come it had been deep and blissful. And then this morning, she'd opened her eyes to the hazy whiteness of mosquito nets and him, sitting there smiling down at her, a jug in his hands…

'*Your hair needs a wash…*'

'*Ah! That explains the jug.*'

'*Of course! Someone told me two days ago that if she was staying at the honeymoon bush camp, then she'd want to replicate the famous hair-washing scene from* Out of Africa, *so here I am, jug and soap at the ready. I also have a poem…*'

'*A poem?*'

'*If it's good enough for Robert Redford…*'

She felt a smile curving on her lips. He'd led her outside, parked her on a warm boulder, leaning her back to wet her hair.

'*I say poem, but it's more of a limerick, really…short and sweet, like your hair.*'

'*A limerick?*'

'I wrote it myself, but don't worry, you're not going to be out a job any time soon.'

'So let's hear it...'

'Okay. There was a young lady called Maddie, who was prone to throwing a paddy, if she was woken up quickly, 'cos it made her quite sickly, or if not sickly, then at least pretty crabby.'

She smiled again, sliding her eyes over his face, feeling the love swelling inside, flowing out. He was everything, the only one she'd ever wanted, the only one who mattered, so why were the jitters coming back, why was she suddenly feeling the weight of her father and everything that went with him—betrayal, shame, fear—pressing down on her, crushing the joy inside? She bit her lips together. Maybe staying was the problem. It wasn't that she didn't want to stay because she did, with all her heart, but staying in one place for more than a few days at a time was counterintuitive. She was a rolling stone, had become one because constant motion was safety. Changing places. Changing faces. It was a decade-old habit, one she was about to break, so maybe that's all it was, nerves chiming because she was about to step out of her comfort zone, but also into one, because that's what Kaden was, what he always had been, her comfort, her joy. *Gah!* She was a bundle of contradictions. No wonder her nerve ends were fraying. If they could just resolve the niggling problem of her name, then maybe it would help.

She took a breath, swallowing hard. 'The thing is, Kade, if we tell them that I'm Maddie Saint James and that we go back a long way, then, given what we've been doing, that's going to make more sense to them than if I'm Lina, who from their point of view has just arrived and within minutes seems to have snagged the boss. If I stay here as Lina, there's a good chance they'll be thinking to themselves that I'm a bit fast and loose, and I'm going to see that in their eyes the whole time and I couldn't bear it because I'm the total opposite, as you well know, but then telling them my real name could be a risk. I'm not saying they'd do it and I feel awful for even thinking it, but as I said before I'm messed up—and this is messed-up me talking—but if they know who I really am, then maybe they might be tempted to contact the press, sell me out for money—'

'Stop!' In one swift movement Kaden had pulled over and switched off the engine. His hand went up, removing hers from the back of his neck. 'Are you listening yourself?' His eyes were bruised, incredulous. 'My staff would never do that. They're like family, a family I pay extremely well for their discretion, and loyalty. I've built Masoka as an exclusive, private venue...' He was shaking his head, his eyes narrowing. 'You know that! We've had travel writers here this week, but my target market is the VIP market—celebrities, politicians—the kind of people who require absolute, one hundred percent discretion. My staff know it, and respect it, so please, don't denigrate them, Maddie. I'm one hundred percent sure of them.'

Even as his words were settling, she could feel words of her own rising from some place deep inside, springing out of her mouth before she could stop them. 'And yet in front of them, right from the first day, you called me *Ms James*, not Maddie, or Ms Saint James, so you can't be *that* sure of them!'

His face stiffened. 'It was *you* I wasn't sure of! That first day I was simply respecting the name you were using. It would have been rather presumptuous of me to start bandying your real name around before we'd even talked about it, don't you think!'

Her heart clenched, then her stomach. He was right. About everything. And she was... She squeezed her eyes shut, sealing in the tears that were suddenly scalding her lids. She was snipped wires. Jagged pieces. She was being unfair, ridiculous. Paranoid.

'I'm sorry.' She bit her lips hard and braved his gaze. Cool. Bruised. She felt her heart buckling, her tears sliding out. 'I'm so sorry… I don't even know where that came from…'

'I do.' His eyes held her for a long second, and then his expression softened. 'You're safe here, Mads. How many more times must I say it?' And then he was moving in, pulling her against him, stroking her hair. 'You need to find some faith.'

She closed her eyes, melting in, feeling the tension inside loosening. So easy having faith when his arms were around her.

His fingers moved to the back of her neck, stroking. 'Anyway, maybe I have a solution for the name thing.'

'What? Calling me crazy?'

He chuckled. 'You are, but no. I'm thinking that if it's going to make you feel better, for now we could go with Lina, and say that it's Lina and I who go back a long way. That way, no one is going to think you're some shady lady. Does that work?'

It was the perfect solution; one she might have thought of herself if she hadn't been so busy spiralling out of control. She felt more tears sliding out, a sudden overwhelming gratitude swelling in her chest. 'It does.' She swallowed hard. 'It's perfect. Unlike me. I'm a mess.'

'You're just scared.' His arms wound around her tighter. 'You've been scared for a long time, but we're going to fix that.' She felt his lips moving in her hair, her heart melting as he whispered, 'I promise.'

'Welcome back, Mr Barr.' Chanda's smile wasn't quite as effusive as usual. *Strange.* Her eyes flicked to Maddie. 'And Ms James... How did you enjoy Tlou?'

'It was wonderful, thank you.' Maddie's eyes came to his briefly. 'I loved every second.' Her cheeks were flushing a little. 'It's quite something being out there, under canvas.'

'It certainly is.' Chanda folded her hands on the reception desk, then folded them again the other way. 'I'm glad you enjoyed it.'

He felt unease stirring. Bad enough Maddie having a little outburst in the car, but at least he got the roots of it, understood where it came from. This low-key, grave-eyed version of Chanda was something else altogether.

'So, Mr Barr...' Chanda's eyes came to his. 'I was wondering if I could have a word.'

'Of course.' The sooner the better. There was something wrong and he needed to know what it was. 'Shall we go into my office?'

'Yes.' She was already moving. 'That would be best.'

'What about me?' The flush in Maddie's cheeks was gone. Now she looked pale. Face. Lips. He felt tension seizing his shoulders. She was clearly thinking that Chanda wanted to talk about *her*. Unlikely, but if he didn't invite her into the conversation, what kind of message was that going to send to her about faith and trust? And what kind of message would it send to Chanda about the relationship between him and Maddie if he didn't ask Maddie to join them? It would create the exact impression that Maddie wanted to avoid, that she'd tempted the boss to a little holiday fling. At least he could nip that one right in the bud.

He held out his arm to her, loading his smile with as much reassurance as he could muster. 'You, too.'

Chanda stalled, her eyes widening. 'Mr Barr?'

'It's fine, Chanda. Lina's a very old friend. Whatever you want to talk to me about, you can say it in front of her.'

Chanda inhaled and then she smiled. 'Of course.'

Moments later, he was closing his office door behind the three of them, feeling the quick hard beats of his pulse bouncing between his temples.

He looked at Chanda. 'So, what is it?'

Her face dropped like a stone. 'It's this...' She went to his desk and picked up a newspaper that hadn't been there when he left, a broadsheet that she battled with for a moment before handing it over, opened out. Her lips pursed. 'It's the *Johannesburg Gazette*.'

He looked, felt his lungs collapsing.

Danger Top of the Menu at Masoka Game Reserve!

He read on, blood roaring, until the words blurred, shifting, and floating on the page. He blinked, forcing himself to read the name of the journalist, even though he already knew: Gerhardus Du Plessis.

'Kaden?' Maddie's anxious voice filtered in, jerking him back. 'What is it?'

He lowered the paper so she could see.

'Oh, my God.' Her eyes flew wide. 'Is that the journalist you sent the champagne to?'

His heart clenched, then his jaw. 'Yes.' He felt an edge drying sharp at the back of his throat. 'And guess what? He even thought to mention it.' He pushed the paper at her and went to the window, staring out blindly.

He hadn't truly got it before, the way his dad had been after the Saint James scandal broke, all those callous-sounding words about for-getting Maddie, about staying away from her and her family for the sake of the business. He hadn't got it then because he'd been seventeen, because he'd been too busy dying inside, but he got it now. His dad would have been thinking of Barr's business reputation and market position, but he must also have been thinking about the staff, their livelihoods, the livelihoods of their suppliers, all the cogs in the Barr's machine, because that's what he was thinking about right now. His staff and their livelihoods, all of which depended on Masoka ranking high, pulling in the right clients, making money. One freak inci-dent, one wretched article! He felt his gut twist-ing. After all his hard work, Fran's hard work, everyone's. Renovating the place to the highest standard, building the lodges, hiring the best chefs, the best guides, the best of every damn thing. The best, most reliable vehicles, the *saf-est* vehicles, which was why Du Plessis was still alive, but he hadn't written that, had he? No. He'd simply dragged Masoka through the dirt and sunk in the boot by mentioning the champagne.

He dragged his hands down his face. He should never have resorted to Dom Pérignon. What had he been thinking? Or maybe that was the problem, he hadn't been thinking. He'd lost his cool, felt panicked, worried for Jerry and the two journalists, worried for the elephant too. He'd been a fizzing ball of overreaction instead of the calm businessman he should have been. Never again.

Next time he'd explain that there was always a degree of danger attached to going out on a game drive, a small risk of injury that was clearly outlined in the terms and conditions. He'd politely and kindly draw their attention to the clause about guests agreeing to participate in game drives at their own risk. And then he'd point out all the different ways that those risks were minimised, via highly competent track-ers and guides, via the constant two-way radio communication between the vehicles so that an-imal movements could be advised, and warn-ings delivered. And he'd emphasise the quality of the vehicles themselves, their stability, and rugged strength. There were cheaper safari ve-hicles available, but he'd bought the best, not skimping, not compromising, because he was his father's son, only interested in delivering quality and satisfaction. And then maybe, once he'd explained all that, he'd offer to add a com-plimentary extra night to the affronted guest's stay, using the time to build back the goodwill.

He sighed. All very well having good ideas

now, but for there to be a next time there needed to be a business. He bit his lips together. He couldn't let this throw him. He couldn't let Du Plessis tilt him off his axis, not now he'd come this far, not when he had staff to think about, plans in motion. Being calm about it, getting things into perspective, what was the reader-ship of the *Johannesburg Gazette* anyway, and the travel section at that? Was the article likely to be syndicated? Maddie would know. Travel was her business after all.

He turned. She was still reading the paper. Did she look paler than before or was it just the light bouncing off the page that was mak-ing it seem that way? He looked at Chanda. Her face was serious, her lips still pursed. He felt a germ of a smile starting, warmth flooding in. Chanda was clearly taking the Du Plessis piece personally. The whole staff would be because as per his earlier conversation with Maddie, they were loyal, invested. They were family. And he wasn't going to let them down by falling apart over this. He was better than that.

He raked a hand through his hair. 'Okay, so maybe it's not the write-up I was hoping for, but we've got eleven more coming right? Have we had any feedback from the journalist who was with Du Plessis?'

'Birgitte Sommer?' Chanda was shaking her

head. 'Not yet, but she's still here. She's leaving tomorrow.'

'Right. Well, hopefully she'll be kinder. When I went to see her, she seemed okay about what happened. Ma—' He bit down on his tongue. Had Chanda noticed his slip? He couldn't bring himself to look. 'Lina?'

'Yes.' Maddie lifted her gaze from the paper, blinking. 'What?'

She looked distracted, stricken around the edges. He felt a knot yanking tight in his belly. If he'd known what Chanda was going to show them, he'd never have included Maddie in the conversation. It was obviously churning her up, feeding her anxiety about journalists. He should let her go, give her an excuse to leave so she wasn't having to hold it together in front of Chanda, but first he needed her opinion.

He went to stand in front of her. 'What do you think the chances are of the article being picked up?'

She shrugged a little. 'He makes some general points about safety in game parks, but there's not enough meat in the article itself to give it real legs.' Her eyes clouded. 'Your biggest problem is the headline. It's hooky so it's going to attract some attention.'

Not what he wanted to hear but at least she was telling him straight. He liked that. What he didn't like were the shadows moving behind her eyes. She was taking this all too hard. Harder than he was. He held in a sigh. The sooner she was all moved in with him the better. Once she was under his wing, he was going take care of her, dedicate himself twenty-four-seven to chasing those shadows away. He was going to bring back the Maddie Saint James sparkle.

'Do you want to go?' He leaned towards her, lowering his voice. 'Pack your stuff.'

If she went to pack now while he was catching up on other business with Chanda—filling Chanda in about him and Maddie—then Tumo would be able to bring up her things.

She nodded. 'Yeah.' Her lips pressed together. 'I'm so sorry about the article.'

'Hey.' He gave her arm a squeeze. 'Don't stress. Really. It'll all be fine.'

She handed him the paper, blinking. 'I hope so.'

She hurried through Reception, head down, heart pounding fit to explode. Why the hell had that damn Du Plessis article gone over the page? If it hadn't, she'd never have seen the other article.

She crashed through the doors and stopped, waiting for the knife to stop twisting. How careful she'd been this week, coming here in the first place, binning the paper that had been left for her every day without even glancing at it, avoiding news sites and social media, and then suddenly, without warning, there it had been right under her nose, a huge smiling picture of her father, a still from some stupid talk show, and that headline: *Where Are You, Madeleine?* What was that even about?

She felt a sob expanding in her chest. As if he was interested! As if he even cared! She squeezed her eyes shut, sucking in a deep breath, forcing her feet to move. But worst of all, *worst of all*, was that picture of herself— inset—a still from the Tresses advert, the one where she'd started off with her hair up in a ponytail, then tugged out the clip so that her hair had tumbled down. Of all the pictures to use, the one with her hair off her face, so that the whole picture was just her face, like a Wanted poster. The only difference between then and now was her hair colour. Anyone at all who saw that picture and who'd seen her without her shades on would join the dots, know for sure that she was Madeleine Saint James. She felt tears burning behind her lids. Nice one, Dad, pulling her back into the spotlight just to blow her cover, exposing her, destroying her all over again. The sob inside struggled upwards, filling her throat. All that hard work, all that steeling herself, pushing through the pain and the panic to create a version of herself, a wary version admittedly, but still a version of herself that was free, able to move through the world on her own terms. And now…

Now Chanda knew, and probably the whole staff too. She'd felt Chanda's eyes on her when she'd turned that page, seen the flicker of acknowledgement there when she'd dared to glance up, and she hadn't been able to say a thing to Kaden, hadn't even been able to signal to him, because he'd been staring through the window, rubbing his head, caught up in his own crisis, thanks to Du Plessis.

She swallowed hard. Poor Kaden. He didn't need all this grief, or the grief she'd given him earlier, implying that his staff might sell her out. Hurt in his eyes. Annoyance. No wonder. Everything he'd said was true. His staff were loyal. She'd seen it for herself, Chanda's obvious chagrin over the article, her demeanour towards Kaden: protective, verging on the maternal. Maybe that's why he'd seemed to rally so quickly, because he knew he had the support of a good team. Maybe that's why, when he'd touched her arm, he'd seemed so grounded. *'Don't you stress. Really. It'll all be fine.'*

She slowed down, lifting her gaze, letting it drift through the tree canopy. Would everything be fine? She breathed in, filling her lungs. The sun was still shining, wasn't it? The sky was still blue. Maybe the Du Plessis article would prove to be a hiccup, nothing more. Maybe the eleven articles to come would knock Du Plessis's piece out of the field. And of course, her piece would count for a lot because her posts always got a lot of traction. So maybe Kaden's faith was well-placed. Which just left her own faith, her own crisis…

She walked on, tuning in to the trilling of the cicadas. The cicadas didn't care if she was Lina or Maddie, they'd keep on trilling anyway. And Chanda, and Precious and Tumo and Jerry, didn't care who she was. They cared about Kaden, and about Masoka, same as her. She touched her pendant, noticing its smoothness. Maybe it didn't matter if her Lina James cover was blown because she was staying here, wasn't she, where it was safe, where she was going to be surrounded by kind, loyal staff. She felt a little lightening sensation around her heart. And now, going for the silver lining, now at least she'd be able to stay as herself, being herself, not worrying about what was going on in London, what her father was saying about his South African co-conspirators. Whistleblowing. Masoka was private, exclusive, respectful. Here, she could be Maddie. Here she could be free.

She felt a sudden springiness in her feet, a smile coming. She *was* free. Free to be with Kaden, free to love him, free to be his support, his port in a storm. Right here, twenty-four seven. She'd help him see off Du Plessis. Maybe she could help him on the website side of things too, writing regular Masoka newsletters, facilitating engagement, building client loyalty. All things she could do in her sleep. Kaden was right. God, he was so right. Everything was going to be fine, was going to be better than—

'Madeleine?'

She froze. Birgitte Sommer. Somehow. There. Phone in hand. Aimed.

'You *are* Madeleine Saint James, aren't you?'

Move! Why weren't her feet moving?

'I'm sorry. You're in shock.' Birgitte's mouth twitched into a tight smile. 'I shouldn't have sprung myself on you like this, but I'm leaving tomorrow, and I'd really like to talk to you. Are you going back to your lodge just now?' Birgitte's eyebrows arched. 'We could walk and talk.'

Walk and talk?

'No!' The word exploded from her mouth, and then suddenly, miraculously, she could feel her limbs again, her feet, feel her blood pumping, strength flowing. She dragged in a breath.

'How dare you. I'm not walking and talking to you, or anyone.' She could hear the hysterical edge on her voice, feel the pain and anger rising, boiling over. 'Just leave me the hell alone. Leave me be.' She aimed a strike at Birgitte's phone, sending it flying, and then she sprinted, running to her lodge, heart pounding and twisting, not looking back.

At the door, she fumbled with the key card, stumbling inside, then fell back, heart pulsing in her throat. How could she have ever thought she'd be free? Safe? She wasn't safe, and she was never going to be free. There was always going to be a Birgitte stepping out in front of her, after a scoop, a headline. She felt her sinuses tingling, tears burning, sliding down her cheeks. And because there was always going to be someone after her, she was never going to find peace, never going to get better. Kaden thought he could fix her, but he couldn't because this was the reality. *Her* reality. Her father had publicly hitched her to his abominable wagon, and it was going to keep rolling and rolling and rolling. She felt her legs giving out, a shudder racking its way through her. He didn't love her enough to be a good man for her, but he wasn't letting her go. She was like Marley, and he was the chain. She was going to be dragging him around for ever, and if she were to stay, then

Kaden was going to be encumbered too, and she wasn't having it. Wasn't. He deserved better. He deserved happiness and success, every good thing in the world. He didn't deserve to be lumbered with a liability such as her.

CHAPTER ELEVEN

'I THINK IT'S wonderful news about you and Ms James.' Chanda's eyes were glowing, full of warmth. 'It doesn't do anyone any good being alone, especially a young man such as yourself.'

At least Maddie wouldn't have to worry any more about anyone thinking she was some kind of predator. As he'd suspected, going off to Tlou had sparked some furious speculation, but he'd given Chanda the bare bones, that they'd been an item in the past, so that was settled.

He smiled. 'Thanks, although frankly I'm not feeling particularly young right now. I messed up with Mr Du Plessis and I seem to be reaping the whirlwind.'

'It'll work out.' Chanda smiled and then suddenly her smile was fading. 'Mr Barr, I want to say something but I'm not quite sure how to say it.'

His heart clenched. Not more difficult news.

He drew in a breath, digging out a smile. 'I always find that straight up is best.'

'Okay, well...' She pursed her lips. 'The thing is, I know—we *all* know—about Ms James, that her name is really Madeleine Saint James.'

He felt the muscles in his face stiffening. 'How?'

Chanda picked up the paper again, thumbing through, and then she turned it round, putting it into his hands.

His heart clenched for a second time, taking his stomach with it.

Peter Saint James was smiling out at him from the page, still handsome in spite of his twelve years inside, and—*Oh, God, no!*—Maddie too, smiling out of a smaller picture, an old Tresses shot, cropped tight. Aside from the dark sideswept fringe, she looked the same. Exactly the same. His slid his eyes up to the headline: *Where Are You, Madeleine?*

His throat went tight. How could Peter have put that in the press, and the photo? He swallowed hard, trying to make his voice work. 'Chanda, did she see this?'

Chanda blinked. 'I think she did, yes.'

No wonder Maddie had looked bleached, stricken. And yet she hadn't said a thing. She'd calmly answered his question about the article, hiding whatever was going on inside, a swan

gliding over a mirror lake, but underneath…
She'd have been melting down, falling apart,
and she'd been doing it alone instead of pouring it all out to him.

He threw the paper down, pulse banging, and
looked at his watch. Nearly a whole hour with
Chanda, going over everything, and all that
time, Maddie had been alone, stewing.

An hour…

His heart seized. It shouldn't have taken her
more than an hour to pack and get back here.
And she wasn't here, was she?

Oh, God!

'Chanda, can you call Tumo, please, right
now? Find out if he's gone to get her bags.'

'Of course.' She bustled out.

He pulled out his phone, swiping and stabbing
at the screen, putting it to his ear. Maybe he was
panicking for nothing. Maybe she'd seen the
picture and was cool. No. On no planet what-
soever was Maddie going to be cool with this.
He paced, holding his breath to the ring-ring,
churning to the endless on-and-on, caving to
the click.

Voicemail.

'Mr Barr—' Chanda was back, eyes wide.
'Tumo did go for her bags, but he put them in
Clive's Jeep. She's gone to the airstrip.'

'No…' His heart was collapsing. This couldn't

be happening. *Couldn't!* Not a second time. He wasn't going to let it happen. He wasn't seventeen any more. She belonged with him. They belonged together. Whatever she was thinking, whatever she thought she was running from, he was going to fight for her, show her that he was there for her whatever it took.

He ducked past Chanda, sprinting through the building, through the doors, running hard until the door of the Land Cruiser was in front of him. He yanked it open, started the engine and stamped on the accelerator, tearing out of the compound, not even braking for Richard's bridge.

She pressed her back into the wall of the little terminal building, clamping her arms to contain the shuddering that wouldn't seem to stop. There were two planes on the apron, two pilots pottering, exchanging the odd word.

She pulled her arms in tighter to quell another shiver. They didn't know she was here. They wouldn't have heard the Jeep because she'd asked Clive to drop her at the back of the building, and not to rev the engine on his way out. And she'd asked him not to tell anyone—*Kaden*—that he'd brought her here until he got back. She'd figured she'd be long gone by then, but for some reason she was still here,

glued to the wall, unable to make her feet take those last steps.

She closed her eyes, feeling the burn. Eyes. Throat. Heart. Why was she stalling? She must get onto one of those planes for Kaden's sake. Staying was only going to taint him by association, bring more Birgittes to Masoka, sniffing around, hunting, and she didn't even understand why, because she was nothing, had nothing to say. She wasn't remotely interesting or important, but they'd keep on coming, keep on tripping her up, making her hateful and angry, and she couldn't inflict that on Kaden as well as everything else, have him suffering her moods and all her paranoia, not after he'd worked so hard to bring Masoka to life. He deserved only the best, because he was best person she knew, the kindest, dearest, most beautiful soul, a beautiful soul who loved her.

She felt her heart buckling, twisting like wreckage. And that was the problem. Now she was here, just metres away from the planes, the thought of leaving him, of actually going through with it, was unbearable. He had so much love inside, so much faith, and she loved him, with every screwed-up fibre of her being.

He'd be there now, wouldn't he, with Chanda, one eye on the door expecting her to walk back in with Tumo and her bags. That's what he was

expecting; meanwhile, she was here, stuck and trembling. *Oh, God!* She felt more tears seeping out, winding down her cheeks. What was she supposed to do? If she got on the plane, she'd be hurting him, and if she went back, she'd be hurting him. It wasn't a choice at all, but she *had* to make a move, push the button, choose the blue or the red—

'Maddie…'

She screwed her eyes tighter, biting her lips. *Maddie, Maddie, Maddie!* That was what he'd be calling out now, going through the guest lounge, feeling worried, maybe striding along the path to her lodge.

'Maddie.' Warm hands gripped her shoulders. 'Maddie. What are you doing?'

She blinked. *Kaden!* Her heart leapt. It was him, really him, right here. His dear face, his beautiful soul, but he shouldn't be here, or— *no*—it was her who shouldn't be here. She should be on the plane. Why hadn't she got on the plane, why couldn't she move, decide, feel anything except this pulsing joy?

'I saw the paper, Mads, your dad, your picture…' He was rubbing her arms gently. 'You should have said something. Why didn't you say something?'

Pain in his eyes. *Her* fault. All her fault.

'I couldn't…' Her voice felt thick in her

mouth, smeary. She swallowed hard. 'You were upset about Du Plessis. You had enough of your own stuff to think about and—' she felt her stomach hardening, darkness closing in '—and I'm sick of everything always being about me and my problems, my stupid dad—'

'But they're not just your problems.' His face was tender. 'They're mine too, because everything that upsets you upsets me, so when something like this happens, I want to know, so we can work through it.' His gaze tightened on hers. 'You don't have to hold it all inside. Maybe your mum never wanted to talk about your dad, but I want you to talk to me. I want to hear it all.' And then he was shaking his head, all the hurt inside showing, the confusion. 'Just taking off like that, without a word, why would you do that to me?' Tears were welling at the edges of his eyes. 'I don't understand. I thought you loved me. I thought we'd agreed—'

She put her hands to his face. 'I do love you, so much.' She bit her lips together hard. 'But then, Birgitte…'

On the path. Tight smile. Phone primed.

'Birgitte what?' His gaze was sharpening, hardening. 'What happened?'

She let her hands fall. 'She accosted me on the way back to the lodge. She was filming me…said she wanted to talk. "Walk and talk,"

she said, as if we were friends, and I—' she felt
a sob rising, filling her throat '—I was so angry,
because of Dad, putting my picture in the paper
like that, inviting all this in again, so I let her
have it. I smashed her phone and ran, and then
I realised that it's never going to stop, whatever
we think, whatever we want, and I was thinking about you and Du Plessis and all the work
you've put in here, and about how if I stay, then
I'm just going to be liability, a hairshirt, always
prickling, irritating, and I don't want that for
you. You deserve better.'

'Oh, Maddie.' He looked away for a beat and
then his eyes fastened on hers. 'Do you know
what I did when your mum told me you'd gone
to Paris?' He ploughed a hand through his hair.
'I followed. I went after you.'

'What?' Her heart pulsed. 'I don't understand… I mean, you didn't even know where I
was staying, so why?'

'Why?' His eyes were blazing suddenly, full
of passion. 'Because I knew you needed me, and
I wanted to be there for you. It's as simple as
that. You're right, I didn't know where you were
staying, but I wanted my love to do some work,
understand? Some actual work. And walking
the streets looking for you was better than just
sitting on my hands.'

She felt her heart turning over, hurting. Even

though he hadn't known where she was, even though it had been a fruitless mission, he'd gone after her, doing the work.

'And it's what I want to do now, more than ever.' He was shaking his head, his gaze softening. 'I don't care what comes. I don't care about your dad, or about the papers, or about Birgitte. I love you, Madeleine Saint James, and my love is strong enough to do the work, to do whatever it takes, because otherwise what does it mean? It's just words.'

Like her dad. Words in the paper, showmanship. Nothing behind it. Nothing real. Nothing there of any worth at all. But Kaden was worth something. He was everything. Maybe it was time to make her love do some work too. Believing in him was a start. Believing in them. She felt warmth filtering in, a fresh warmth that felt hopeful and pure.

He was taking her face in his hands, wiping her tears with gentle thumbs, and then suddenly he was smiling. 'For the record, if you're a hairshirt, then I can't wait to slip you on, but we'll have to go back to my place for that.' His lips came to hers for a long moment, warm and firm, drawing a tingle through her veins. 'What do you say?'

His place. His home. Hers now too. No more doubts. No more running.

She felt tears budding and spilling and then a smile arriving. 'I'm saying, yes. I'm saying, sorry. I'm saying, Kaden Barr, I love you with all my heart. And I'm saying, please, take me home.'

EPILOGUE

Six months later...

'WHAT HAVE YOU got so far?' Birgitte was looking at her with that funny little tight-lipped smile of hers, a smile that was apt to widen and brighten in a heartbeat, or equally, to draw tight, depending on the circumstances.

She toyed with the notebook in her lap. 'Not much, but I have been rather busy...'

'Excuses, excuses...' Birgitte picked up her glass, chuckling. 'Anyone would think you'd been organising a wedding...'

She felt a smile coming. *Birgitte!* Who'd ever have thought that they'd become firm friends? Letters of apology simultaneously crossing via the reception desk, hers apologising for smashing Birgitte's phone; Birgitte's apologising for the way she'd approached her on the path. From there, somehow, things had progressed. A few weeks and scores of emails later, Birgitte had finally persuaded her that writing her own story would be good for her, cathartic. And Kaden had agreed. But then he'd proposed, which had taken her eye off the ball just a little bit.

She felt a lump thickening in her throat. Tomorrow, she was marrying the love of her life on the veranda where they'd had that first dinner all those months ago. Just a small wedding, which, in truth, hadn't taken that much organising. Mum was here, and Renée, and Kaden's parents and his sister and her boyfriend. Grandma Barr too. They were all outside on the front veranda with Kaden, drinking sundowners. She could picture his face, his eyes full of delight, his ready smile, pride in it. Masoka was doing so well. The Du Plessis blip, which is what they called it now, had been short-lived. The other reviews, and her own, had brought those first bookings in, and the now the ball was not so much rolling as careening full speed ahead. Nothing less that he deserved.

Kaden. Her rock, her shelter, her safety. Her one and only love. For ever. He'd probably be looking about him now, wondering where she was. Would he be feeling a twitch of anxiety in some corner of his beautiful soul? It hurt that he might be, but if he was, then it was all down to her. She was better than she had been, better by a mile, but it was still there inside from time to time, that jumping anxiety, and Kaden knew. Because he *knew* her, all her snipped wires and jagged pieces, and he loved her all the same.

'So are you going to read it out or what…?' Birgitte's eyebrows were at maximum elevation.

She looked down at the notebook. She didn't need to open it to know what it held.

My father's name is Peter Christian Saint James. I grew up thinking he was a good man, a kind and honest man. In truth, I idolised him as if he were, indeed, a saint. The hardest lesson of my life was learning that he was the opposite. This is my story…

She swallowed hard, meeting Birgitte's curious gaze. 'No, it can wait…' She put the notebook aside and got to her feet. 'But Kaden can't. He'll be wondering where I am, and I can't have that, not on the night before our wedding…'

Birgitte set down her glass and then she was looking up, her eyes full of warmth and shine. 'You really do love him, don't you?'

She felt her heart filling, exploding softly. 'Oh, Birgitte, you have no idea.'

* * * * *

If you enjoyed this story, check out these other great reads from Ella Hayes

The Single Dad's Christmas Proposal
Tycoon's Unexpected Caribbean Fling
Unlocking the Tycoon's Heart
Italian Summer with the Single Dad

All available now!